# O the Red Rose Tree

Mrs. Hankinson said, "I been thinkin' about a certain quilt ever since I was a bride sixty-three years back."

Jessy asked, "What's it called?"

"O the Red Rose Tree."

"There's an 'O' in it?" Pheemie was puzzled.

"Euphemia, if I say there's a 'O' in it, there is one. I'm makin' up the pattern, so it's mine to name."

I was excited. "Then it's a pattern nobody ever saw before. It'd be a brand-new quilt!"

Mrs. Hankinson nodded at me. "If it ever was to be, it would be somethin' new. But it's just a idea I had. I can't make it, girls."

"Why not?" asked Pheemie.

"Because it'll have seven roses—seven red ones, mostly all diff'runt shades of red. . . . When I couldn' find the seven true-color reds I wanted and could afford to get, even down in Frisco stores that had bolts and bolts a cotton, I just give up. I found five of 'em there I fancied, but they cost too much money. That Europe-made cloth comes mighty dear."

"Do you remember your pattern for the quilt?" Molly asked her.

"Oh, girl, now would I forget that?"

"Then go ahead and make the quilt! Amanda and Jessy and Pheemie and I—we'll find the reds you need!"

*for Jacqueline*

*Who made Nachotta
and Oysterville more than
names in a book.*

# O the

# Red Rose Tree

*May this give you the
pleasure it gave me.*

## PATRICIA BEATTY

*Love
Patti*

A Beech Tree Paperback Book ✦ New York

First published in 1972 by William Morrow and Company, Inc. Reissued in
hardcover by Morrow Junior Books and in paperback by Beech Tree Books in
1994 with minor changes that update the text for a contemporary audience.
Printed in the United States of America. First Beech Tree Edition, 1994.
10 9 8 7 6 5 4 3 2 1

Library of Congress Cataloging-in-Publication Data
Beatty, Patricia.
    O the red rose tree / Patricia Beatty.
        p.   cm.
    Summary: In 1893 four girls befriend an old lady and try to find seven shades
of red for the special quilt she wants to make.
    ISBN 0-688-13627-3
    [1. Friendship–Fiction.]   I. Title.
PZ7.B3805440al   1994
[Fic]—dc20                                                              93-50232
                                                                            CIP
                                                                            AC

# Contents

1  *The Old Witch in the Silver Shack*                    1

2  *Grandma Goes Calling!*                               18

3  *The Impossible Begins*                               36

4  *Flotsam*                                             52

5  *Maud Williams*                                       71

6  *News from Portland*                                  91

7  *Out Among the Nabobs*                               109

8  *High Water!*                                        131

9  *Bellini*                                            153

10  *A Real Red Red!*                                   174

*Author's Note*                                        194

# O the Red Rose Tree

# 1

## The Old Witch in the Silver Shack

MOLLY AND JESSY came running so fast up to my front porch that they were holding their skirts up over their knees. They knew better. What if Grandma Barnett saw them? You could bet that quicker'n I could say "scat," she'd be out to blister their ears. It didn't matter if any girl she caught showing her knees "out in public" was a relation to us or not, Grandma would let her have it.

I looked over my shoulder to see if she was standing there behind me, waiting to pounce, but only Horace, my baby brother, and Edward T. Bone, our old dog, were on the porch with me.

"Hey, Amanda Ann, guess what?" Molly skidded to a stop in the sand in our front yard with Jessy right behind, breathing down her neck.

"Yes, guess what?" Jessy repeated.

I was exasperated. They'd waked up Horace, who was horrible because he was teething. I said, "Rats!" then lifted him out of his cradle to shush him. "What is it? Where's Pheemie?" Pheemie was always with Molly and Jessy.

Molly was so out of breath she could hardly talk. "Phee-mie's down keeping watch for us on the old witch!"

"Huh? What witch?" Molly's cheeks were rose-pink, and her brown bangs stuck out frizzy from running.

"The one who lives in the silver shack," said Jessy, panting. Jessy's hair was almost as yellow as mine, and her great big eyes were a darker blue than mine, but I wasn't jealous because she was my friend. Besides, I was getting plumper much faster in the right places, now that we had all turned thirteen.

"The silver shack!" I said scornfully. "Grandma told me it's been empty for years and years since Mr. Hankinson who built it went away and never came back. We weren't even born yet when he left. And the shack isn't really silver at all. It just never got painted, and the ocean air and sun turned the wood gray."

Molly cried out, "Well, there's somebody there now! We saw her. An old lady, a witch with a long nose and pointed chin in a long black dress!"

I heaved a sigh as Horace started to yell and hit me in the face with his fists. "Now see what you did, Molly Stevens. You know I have to look after Horace Saturday mornings when Pa and Mama go to Oysterville to the store. It isn't easy when he's teething." I rocked back and forth on the top step with my brother, singing to him.

"Amanda Ann Barnett, there is, too, a witch!" Jessy interrupted my lullaby.

"Oh, rats, Jessamine Reed. There aren't such things as witches." I'd read as many books as she had, almost every single one on the Peninsula we could get our hands on. "This is Washington State in 1893, not Salem, Massachusetts, in the 1600s."

Molly looked a little bit doubtful. "But, Amanda, the old witch sure looks like one."

"Does she have a broomstick or a black pointed hat?"

Molly shook her braids. "No, but she's got a black cat, a great big one. That ought to prove something."

I said over my shoulder to Edward T. Bone, "Get up and show them you're a big black dog." He didn't, of course. He moved only when Grandma Barnett poked him with her cane or a flea bit him or we waved a piece of meat in front of his nose.

"Pheemie thinks it's a witch down at the silver shack, too," Jessy piped up. "The witch was hanging out clothes on one side of some Scotch broom bushes. We got a real good look at her from the other side. Pheemie's still down there on guard."

That sounded like Pheemie, who was the biggest and the bravest of us four eighth-graders. "Well, what do you want me to do about the witch?" I asked.

"Come down with us and spy on her too."

I looked at Horace. What was I going to do with him? He was too heavy to lug around for very long. Then I remembered that Allan was home. I gave Horace to Molly to hold and went around the side of our house to the barn. My big brother was lying on some hay bales, his arms folded under his head, looking up at the loft. I guessed he was thinking of the square dance in Oysterville that night and all the Peninsula girls who were frizzing up their hair with hot curling irons they'd stuck inside lamp chimneys. They'd be hoping to be waltzed around by him. Allan was twenty-one, the best swimmer and dancer and "laziest oaf in the whole state," according to Grandma Barnett. I thought he was good-natured.

"Allan, I need you to mind the baby for a while."

He moved slow as ever. The two of us got along fine. He never asked me why I wanted things. He usually just did them—or didn't do them.

Our house was a big yellow one with balconies upstairs and pillars out front. Because we lived so close to the ocean and the winter storms were pretty bad, our porches were deep to keep out the blowing sand. It took a little while for Allan and me to get around the side of the house and up onto the porch to take Horace away from Molly.

"He's wet!" said Molly, her face deep pink. I didn't know whether she was blushing because Horace was wet or because she was stuck on Allan. Girls thought he was handsome because he was so strong and had curly thick brown hair, white teeth, and sunburnt skin. He had an awful effect on ladies.

"Where you gals going?" he asked, as he sat down on the step next to Edward T. Bone, whose head was hanging over the edge of the porch between two railings.

"Down to rescue Pheemie Sharp from the clutches of a witch," I told him.

"Uh-huh, Halloween is coming up," was all he said. Then he started talking to Horace, who was blowing bubbles into his face.

* * *

MOLLY, WALKING BESIDE ME on the Nahcotta road, sighed like a suck hole in a creek. "Golly, he's handsome. He doesn't look a bit like you, Amanda."

"Thank you very, *very* much."

"You look like maybe Grandma Barnett used to look a million years ago," came from Jessy.

"Thank *you* very much, Jessy!" I stopped in my tracks. "Maybe I'm not going with you after all. Maybe I don't want to go spying on witches today. Maybe I've got something better to do, like looking at stereopticon slides of 'The Glory That Was Greece,' or cutting my toenails or playing the piano. . . ."

I was getting good and wound up when I heard a voice screeching behind me, "Amanda! Amanda Ann Barnett!"

I froze, then turned around. There was Grandma Barnett out on the front porch, leaning on her cane. I didn't budge when she called again, for I could see that Allan was talking to her, sweet-talking her, I bet. He was the only one in the house who could get his way with her. Not even Pa, her own son, could tone her down. Mama had been buffaloed from the start. Grandma ruled the Barnett roost, which half the Peninsula said wasn't a natural thing for an old hen to do. I watched while she went back inside the house, slamming the screen door. Then Allan waved at me to go on. I went fast, but not until I'd seen poor Edward T. Bone slink down off the porch and across the road toward the beach.

"Ha!" said Jessy, who walked next to me in the wagon rut in the sand. "You say there aren't any witches, huh?"

"Oh, you be quiet, Jessamine." I wouldn't discuss my grandmother with them, because I'd only get more upset.

We were all quiet for a while, and then Dr. Alf Perkins came along in his buggy on the way to Oysterville. He stopped so we could pat his old horse, Rosinante.

"Are you on an errand of mercy?" I asked him.

"I am going to visit a patient, if that is what you call an errand of mercy, Amanda." He tipped his derby hat to each of us, looked at his watch, which played "The Blue Danube" waltz, clucked to Rosinante, and went on down the road.

"That Rosinante must be fifty years old at least," said Jessy. "Dr. Alf ought to get himself a new horse."

"Dr. Alf doesn't ever want to get anything new," I told her. "Mama thinks that's why he never got married and keeps on living at the Palace Hotel in Nahcotta. Pa says the doctor likes 'single blessedness.' He could have married any lady anywhere if he'd wanted to."

THE OLD HANKINSON PLACE was just outside of Nahcotta, which was about a mile from our house. We went to school in Nahcotta, so every day I walked by the Hankinson shack, though I couldn't really see it because it was down behind some sand dunes.

"How'd you know somebody was living there?" I asked Molly and Jessy when we were up close.

"We were going to Pheemie's house when we saw the smoke coming out of the chimney," Jessy explained. "We were on an eerie walk."

I knew all about the eerie walks in the early morning. I

liked them, too, especially when the four of us went prowling around the old abandoned homesteads up around Oysterville. Grandma Barnett and Mama didn't like the idea—they were scared we'd fall into the old wells. They got even more upset when we explored the old wrecks of ships at low tide on the ocean beach.

Jessy flopped down on top of the sand dune that overlooked the Hankinson place. "Come on, you two. This is the way Hawkeye does in *The Last of the Mohicans* when he's spying on the Hurons in the wilds."

Without making a sound, the three of us slithered over the top of the high sand dune and slid down to the bottom, where there were lots of tall Scotch broom bushes. I saw the washing on the bushes, spread out to dry, but it was a real funny one. There were no petticoats or corset covers or towels, only pieces of percale and muslin and calico in all colors and sizes and shapes. I poked Molly and whispered, "Hey, where's Pheemie supposed to be?"

Jessy hissed at me, "This is where we left her. She's gone!"

I was beginning to get a little bit scared now. This was really an eerie walk. Pheemie should have stayed put, and that laundry on the bushes was pretty weird. I wanted to say that maybe we ought to run to Nahcotta for help, but before I could get the words out, Molly prodded me in the ribs.

"Look, there's the old witch!"

Molly had her head stuck through a bush. I stuck mine next to hers and so did Jessy. We didn't breathe at all. The elderly lady who lived in the tumbledown gray shack

looked like a witch all right. She had gray hair in a bun, a
pale wrinkled face, a long nose, and a sharp chin. Her dress
was all black without even a white collar. She walked pretty
straight but kind of stiff, which didn't fit. Witches leaned
on canes and were bent over in all the pictures I'd ever
seen. But they did have cats, and behind the old woman
walked the biggest black cat I ever saw. He must have
weighed at least twenty pounds.

"That's her familiar!" Jessy whispered.

For a second I thought the witch had heard Jessy because
she came straight toward us, making me wish I could burrow into the sand like a razor clam. But she stopped on
the other side of the bush and felt a piece of cloth to see
if it was dry.

We watched her like Hawkeyes. Shielding her eyes with
her hand, she looked up into the sky, bright blue and full
of white gulls flying around in circles. Next she walked to
another bush to feel another piece of cloth. Then we heard
her start singing. Her voice was quivery.

Oh, who's goin' to shoe your pretty little foot,
Oh, who's goin' to glove your hand-ee-o,
Oh, who's goin' to kiss your red-rosy lips,
When I'm in that furrin land-ee-o?

She went back toward the shack, still singing.

Oh, it's call in a fine carpenter,
It's make a ship for me-o,

For I must seek out Lovin' George
Wherever he can be-o.

As she opened the door of the shack, she said to the cat, "Come in now, Jocelyn."

I looked at Jessy and Molly, surprised. That was a funny name for a familiar.

Molly put her finger to her lips, backed out from under the bush, and started to crawl on her hands and knees between the other bushes. As she went, she made seagull sounds, the signal we used to call each other. The gulls were never fooled, but people were. Jessy and I went scuttling like crabs after Molly, coming to a halt under a window of the silver shack—one that wasn't broken.

Quick as a flash Molly jumped up and peeked in, her face white as cottage cheese. It was bright red when she crouched down. "Oh, that Euphemia!" she squeaked.

"What'd the old witch do to her?" Jessy wanted to know. "Did she pop Pheemie into the oven like witches do?"

"No!" Molly was mad enough to sizzle. "Pheemie's sitting at the table stuffing herself." Now Molly's face changed back to white again as she grabbed her braids and held them straight up in the air to show how horrified she was. "Eating in a witch's house puts a person in the power of the witch forever and ever!" she gasped.

"Rats!" I said. "Euphemia Sharp just loves eating." Grandma Barnett told me once that if the stage wasn't such a "wicked, scarlet calling," Molly Stevens ought to become an actress, she put so much melodrama into everything she did. I jumped up to look into the silver shack myself.

There sat Pheemie, her black hair up in green ribbons, jamming her face with biscuits from a tin in front of her. I guess I moved too fast and caught her eye, because she looked right at me, pointed to her stuffed face, and crooked her finger for me to come inside.

I popped down again. "We've been seen!"

"By the witch?" asked Jessy.

"No, by Pheemie. She wants us to come in."

Molly exploded, "And be in the power of a wicked witch forever and ever!"

"Rats, Molly! There are no witches. She's only an old lady. Pheemie looks fine, and she's eating biscuits. I'm going." I got up, brushed the sand from my shoes and skirt and apron, and went to the door. From there I gave the others a fierce look. "Well, what about you two Hawkeyes? Are you coming or are you running away?"

They got up mighty slowly, but they came to the door. I knocked.

Pheemie opened the door. Swallowing what she had in her mouth, she said, "Mrs. Hankinson's making some mint tea. Come in and meet her. She just moved in two days ago."

I stood in the doorway and peered around. The place didn't look much to me as if anybody really had moved in properly yet. Boxes and baskets and trunks lay all over the floor next to the rusty pot-bellied stove. There were dishes in a cupboard made out of two big crates set on top of each other and four unpainted chairs set at a big golden oak table and braided rag rugs on the swept floor. A teakettle was boiling on top of the stove.

Mrs. Hankinson, as Pheemie had called her, was standing over the teakettle. She smiled at me and nodded, while Jessy poked me in the back, whispering, "Amanda, get out of the doorway."

We all came inside, and Mrs. Hankinson said, "How d'ya do, girls."

I never did know what to say to "How do you do?" The question was silly. Jessy answered, "Hello," but Molly was still too scared to say a word. The cat saved me as he came walking up and rubbed, purring, against my ankles. I reached down and patted him.

"He's named Jocelyn," said Pheemie.

"I have a dog that's all black," I told Mrs. Hankinson when I straightened up.

"He's named Edward T. Bone," added Molly.

"We used to have a all-black horse, but we haven't got her anymore since she stepped on Pa's foot," said Jessy.

"Black animals are mighty handsome most of the time," the old lady said calmly. "Set yourselves down, girls, and have some tea." She waved toward the chairs. When we didn't sit down right away, she smiled. "There ain't nothin' to be scared of. I won't put you under a spell so you'll wake up a hundred years from now with long gray beards."

I gave Pheemie my dirtiest look, thinking she'd tattled to the old lady that we thought she was a witch. But Pheemie shook her head—no, she hadn't.

Mrs. Hankinson, who'd watched us, laughed—not a witch cackle at all, but a real laugh. "Yep, I'm somethin' of a mind reader. Lots of old folks get to be. And then I *did* see you three out under the bushes, like I saw Euphemia a while back." When she turned away to take down some teacups, we sat down. Molly, Jessy, and Pheemie had chairs, but I sat on an empty box so Mrs. Hankinson would have a chair.

"I can tell you're Amanda," the old lady said to me, as she put dried mint leaves into a teapot on the table.

"How'd you guess?" Molly asked. I was too speechless.

"Oh, Euphemia described all of you to me and said you'd be comin' right along to visit, too. Amanda's the one who gen'rally minds her manners." She cocked her head to one side and eyed Molly. "You'd be Molly. You're the one that hankers after excitement and has pink cheeks." Her eyes, bright blue, not black the way a witch's should be, took in Jessy next. "Jessamine dreams dreams and likes big words."

I thought it was darned nice of Pheemie to tell only the good things about us, so I said as my tea was being poured, "Euphemia knows an awful lot about animals. She wants to be a horse doctor."

Mrs. Hankinson sat down and shoved the tin box of biscuits in front of Pheemie over to me. One after the other we each took a biscuit and ate it. They were plain old biscuits, not a single magic thing about them. For a while it was so quiet the only thing I could hear was the cat's purring on Mrs. Hankinson's lap. To break the silence, I asked her, "Are you related to the Hankinson who built this house?"

"He was my youngest boy. He died last year down in Frisco."

"That's San Francisco, in California," Pheemie explained. "Her oldest son died of quinsy in 1850. The next one got killed in a battle in the Civil War, and she never did have any girls. Mr. Hankison died back East in Kentucky in 1847 of consumption. Mrs. Hankinson's eighty years old now. Her birthday was in September. She came up here when her youngest son died, because he left her this shack in his will. She didn't have 'chick nor child' anymore in the whole wide world, only this old place, so she packed up and came here." Pheemie took a deep breath, grinning.

I felt like asking her if she'd found out yet whether Mrs. Hankinson's teeth were store-bought, but instead I turned towards Mrs. Hankinson and asked, "Did you ever live on the Peninsula before?"

"No, Amanda. When my son was up here I was livin' alone back in Kentucky. I never been in Washington State till now, but he'd been most everywhere." She sighed a little and folded her hands in her lap. "All his movin' around musta come from my puttin' the Wanderin' Foot on his bed when he was a little boy."

"The Wandering Foot?" Molly asked.

"Yes, the quilt that makes a rollin' stone outa any boy who sleeps under it."

I saw how Jessy's eyes were gleaming. She had some pesky brothers all right, the kind who would put burrs in church pews before the choir sat down.

Pheemie started in again. "And her son who died down

in Frisco never had any kids when he was married. So she hasn't got any grandchildren either."

I ignored Pheemie. After all, Mrs. Hankinson was a closer neighbor to us Barnetts than to the Sharps, who lived south of Nahcotta beside the railroad tracks. "Will you be staying here long?" I asked Mrs. Hankinson.

She sipped some tea and nodded. "I think so, child. I'm tired of pickin' up and puttin' down." Then she frowned and reached for the old red wool shawl draped on the back of Pheemie's chair and put it over her shoulders. "I only just got here, but I'm not too sure the ocean air's goin' to be good for what ails me. This is wetter'n Frisco. But I can't keep on—"

"What ails you?" Jessy busted in.

"Arthritis, Jessamine."

I knew about arthritis. Dr. Alf had a touch of it, too. I'd heard him complain to Mama about it when he came to our house the times we were sick. He loved to tell Mama everything that was wrong with him.

Then Molly came out with, "What is it you can't keep on doing? You didn't finish what you were saying. Jessy didn't let you."

"Movin' around. Have another biscuit, Molly. The truth of it is that I haven't got the money to make another move, and I'm just bone weary of it."

"You're poor, huh?" asked Jessy.

"Oh, she's real, real poor," Pheemie told Jessy.

"Are you starving to death?" asked Molly.

"No, I won't starve," Mrs. Hankinson said. "The money

I have oughta last as long as I do. After all, I'm old as the itch!"

Mrs. Hankinson didn't seem to notice that I was hot all over because I was so embarrassed. The way we were all talking in front of her was awful. I figured she was poor, and I'd found out that she was the oldest lady on the Peninsula, beating Grandma, who prided herself on being the oldest at seventy-six. But we ought to let up on the questions.

Jessy kept right at it. "How'd you get up here?"

"By ship to Astoria, across the Columbia River on a boat, and then up to here on your little railroad." I frowned at that last remark. I was proud of our narrow gauge railroad that ran from Ilwaco down near the Columbia River to Nahcotta. Mrs. Hankinson seemed to know I was mad, because she put her hand over mine and squeezed it. "What's your middle name, Amanda?"

"Ann."

I thought she looked happy to hear it. "That'd be mine, too, honey. My name's Sarah Ann."

We talked for a while about Oysterville and Nahcotta and about our sisters and brothers. When the tea was all gone, I kicked Molly under the table as a signal, and said, "It's time we took our leave."

"You come again, girls." Mrs. Hankinson went to the door with us.

"We'll come," I promised. I liked her a lot.

Molly promised more. "And we'll bring you some clams we dug on the beach."

"And some crabs," added Jessy.

"And fish, too, from Willapa Bay." Pheemie was a good fisherman.

All of my friends were looking at me. What could I bring? It had to be special, since I was the last one to offer. Pa sold our eggs and milk and cream in Oysterville, so it couldn't be any of those things. Then I saw all the boxes on the floor filled with pieces of cloth. Jocelyn had gone to sleep on a scrap of yellow muslin rag.

Mrs. Hankinson saw me looking and chuckled. "Did you girls ever notice that a cat always curls up on a color that sets him off good? Jocelyn never goes to sleep on purple or dark blue."

I smiled and said, "My big brother Allan'll make you a real clothesline. We've got plenty of old rope in our barn." Also I'd noticed some pine trees the right distance apart for clothes poles behind the silver shack.

"Why, that's just about the nicest thing anyone ever promised me, Amanda," Mrs. Hankinson said, as she shut the door behind us.

We climbed up the sand dune and stopped in the middle of the road out of sight of the shack.

"Golly, she's poor as a church mouse," Molly said.

"I bet that was her supper we ate," Jessy added.

I was pretty sure it was too, but didn't say so. We shouldn't have gobbled all those biscuits.

What Pheemie said was, "Mrs. Hankinson's sure nice. You know, she didn't treat us like kids at all. She treated us like grown-ups."

I said good-bye and headed north, while Pheemie and

Jessy headed south toward Nahcotta, and Molly went west to Klipsan Beach and the Life Saving Station, where her pa was an officer.

I guessed we were all thinking how bad off Mrs. Hankinson was as we walked home. Up on the Peninsula money was always scarce as hen's teeth, but it seemed to me she must have less of it than anyone else I ever had heard of.

There was something else about her too. She was sort of mysterious, even if she wasn't a witch. Why did she have all those pieces of cloth that looked like rags scattered around? There must have been dozens and dozens of them.

# 2

## Grandma Goes Calling!

Halfway home I ran into Dr. Alf coming back from Oysterville. He tipped his hat to me again, but might not have reined in Rosinante if I hadn't grabbed the bridle and stopped her.

"What's the matter, Amanda?" he asked.

"Dr. Alf, there's a brand-new old lady living down in the sand dunes outside of Nahcotta."

He smiled. "That's a funny way to put it. How can there be a brand-new old lady?"

"Well, there is. Her name is Mrs. Hankinson. She's eighty years old, she lives in the old Hankinson shack, and she's got arthritis, too, just like you have."

I thought Dr. Alf pursed his lips, but his big, drooping yellow moustache was in the way, so I couldn't be sure. "You can tell her for me then that she picked a dang-fool place to come to. Tell her to try the Mojave Desert—not the beach."

"Oh, I wouldn't do that. She's sort of odd, but we like her. We don't want her to move away before we get to know her good. Will you go see her about her arthritis?"

"No, Amanda." Dr. Alf gave me his sternest take-your-medicine look. "I'll go to Mrs. Hankinson, of course, if she sends for me—or her son does."

"Her son's dead. She's alone. Dr. Alf, did you know her son who built the shack? She said he had a 'wandering foot.' "

He nodded. "Yes, I knew him when he was up here. He had not only wandering feet but wandering wits, if you ask me—one of the most worthless men who ever drew breath. Now, Amanda, you unhand my horse so I can get back to Nahcotta in time to keep my office hours."

I let go of Rosinante's bridle and petted her neck again. "Well, I'll sure put in a good word for you with Mrs. Hankinson in case she ever gets sick," I told the doctor.

"You do that for me, Amanda. I will appreciate it very much. Please be sure to inform her, too, that I am the only doctor between here and Ilwaco and Oysterville."

"Oh, I'll tell her all right."

This time he didn't tip his hat to me. He drove off with Rosinante stumbling along down the middle of the road, keeping the buggy wheels in the ruts. I stood for a while looking after them, wondering if maybe Rosinante had arthritis too. Pheemie had said more than once that the old mare was about to come down with the heaves.

When I got home, I found Allan and Horace gone, but Grandma Barnett was sitting in her rocking chair on the porch. She was stabbing her crochet hook so fast in and out of the antimacassar she was making that I knew she was mad as a hornet again. The madder Grandma got the faster her fingers went at whatever she was doing, even brushing snarls out of my hair. She gave me a sharp look from over the top of her spectacles, then said, "All right, my girl, where have you been? Why did you run off when I called you?"

To head her off, I threw her a piece of news. "Down visiting a new neighbor of ours, Grandma."

That stopped her the way I'd hoped it would. She even put down the antimacassar. "New neighbor? Who'd that be? Nobody told me."

"Mrs. Hankinson."

"Somebody's living down in that dreadful old shack that Hankinson built?"

"Yes'm."

She snorted. "I knew young Hankinson. He was a youth of no consequence if ever I saw one. Probably there's bad blood in the family that produced him. I suppose his wife has come up here with him to live in that awful place?"

"No, Grandma. It's his mother. He died."

"His *mother*! Why would she come from anyplace to live in that shack?"

I didn't want to tell her how poor Mrs. Hankinson was, so I only said, "Maybe she wanted some sea air."

Grandma snorted again. "With winter coming on! Don't be silly, girl. How old would you say she is?"

"She told Pheemie Sharp she was eighty."

Grandma clicked her false teeth together. She looked annoyed. "Older than I am! Well, go on. Tell me what she's like."

I sat down on the porch as she started on her crocheting again. I knew that the antimacassar was for my hope chest, ready for the day somebody married me. The cedar chest at the foot of my bed was full of all kinds of junk already. Pa said I'd had enough to set up housekeeping when I was ten years old—embroidered dish towels, crocheted tablecloths, pillowcases with tatting lace, bed sheets with cutwork tops, and three bed quilts too. When I'd wanted dolls for Christmas, I got tea towels instead from Grandma.

"Oh, Mrs. Hankinson's wonderful. She made mint tea for Molly and Pheemie and Jessy and me. She gave us biscuits, and sings songs about somebody named Lovin' George and 'kissing red-rosy lips,' and hangs her laundry on the Scotch broom bushes."

"Good heavens!" Grandma missed a loop in her crocheting. "She must be in her second childhood or weak in the head. That's ghastly!"

I giggled before I told her, "The song was about shoes and gloves, and she dried cloth on the bushes because she hasn't got a real clothesline yet." I thought a minute before I said, "After all, she only moved in the other day. Doesn't doing a washing so soon prove she's awful clean? We liked her a lot."

The last remark made her sniff, as I figured it might. She said nothing for a while, only rocked faster, then announced, "Tomorrow's Sunday. After church you and I will go calling on Mrs. Hankinson. I'd like to meet this paragon who sings songs about kissing and does hedge laundries."

I hadn't planned to go back to the silver shack again until next Saturday with Allan along to rig up the clothesline. "I was just there, Grandma!"

"No matter, Amanda. You know her, so you can introduce me. It's my Christian duty to welcome her. Perhaps I'll even invite her into the Methodist Church's sewing circle."

I gave in. What else could I do? If Mrs. Hankinson got tied up right off with the ladies in Oysterville, she probably wouldn't be interested in visits from us eighth-graders anymore. I got up and went inside the house to find Mama and tell her about our new neighbor.

She was in the kitchen sifting flour onto a piece of paper, which meant she was going to make a cake. She'd already made bread this week.

"Mama, there's a poor, elderly lady living down in the Hankinson place. Grandma and I are going calling on her tomorrow afternoon. Will you come too?"

Mama finished her sifting before she answered. "I can't go. The preacher and his wife are invited to supper tomorrow night. I'll have too much to do. You and Grandma can represent the family without me."

Well, my hash was fried to a crisp all right. I'd hoped Mama would come along. Sometimes a third party could take the edge off Grandma. I couldn't ask Pa or Allan—men never went calling Sunday afternoons. They sure were luckers sometimes. What's more, if the preacher and his wife came to dinner, they'd bring John with them. He was my most unfavorite boy in the world. John Pratt and Grandma would absolutely ruin Sunday!

GRANDMA BARNETT made me wear my scratchy blue serge sailor dress and a black bow in my hair. She dolled up, too, in her black silk and her paisley shawl with all the blues and greens in it. Everybody admitted that she was a "fine figure of a woman," big and "well-preserved," but then they didn't have to live with her.

We went calling in style. Pa took us in our buggy as far as we could go. Then we went down over the sand dune with me watching my way so I wouldn't fall down with my basket and break the jar of wild strawberry jam or squash Mama's piece of cake.

"Dear me!" Grandma stopped at the bottom of the dune to look at the Hankinson shack. "It certainly has gone to wrack and ruin, Amanda."

I had hoped that seeing it would make her turn back, but she went right up to the front door and knocked.

Mrs. Hankinson seemed surprised and puzzled to see Grandma Barnett. Then she turned to me and said, "Well, hello again, Amanda Ann."

"This is my grandmother, Mrs. Hankinson. She's named Mrs. Barnett. We've come to call."

As we went inside I saw how my grandmother took everything in with one beady-eyed look. Things still were pretty messy at Mrs. Hankinson's. Grandma wrinkled up her nose to sniff the way she did when our parlor needed tidying, but she held it back.

"I'll make some tea. Set yourself down, Mrs. Barnett," said Mrs. Hankinson.

Grandma walked around the golden oak table, testing the old chairs by jerking the backs until she found the steadiest one. Plunking herself down, she pointed with her cane for me to put the basket on the table. "We've brought you some jam and some cake," she told Mrs. Hankinson. "I'm sure you could use—"

I burst in fast. "Pheemie and I picked the strawberries for the jam. They're the little, tiny wild ones that grow in the sand. You have to pick hundreds and hundreds of them to make just one cup of jam. I—"

Grandma thumped her cane on the floor. "Amanda, you're chattering. Sit down and mind your manners."

As I sat down Mrs. Hankinson said softly, "I think Amanda has magnificent manners. Her friends seem to think so too."

"Bah!" Grandma snorted. "Young girls nowadays are nothing but flibbertigibbets. They have nothing but high animal spirits."

While I stared at my hands and Mrs. Hankinson took down a can of tea, Grandma looked around the place some more. Then suddenly she drew herself up rigid as a poker. "Is that a *cat* I see lying in that basket in the corner?"

I knew how Grandma felt about animals, except for the useful ones like cows and horses and hens, so I said, "I think he's the prettiest, biggest, blackest cat I ever saw."

Now she really let go. "I despise cats. They are shiftless, worthless, deceitful animals. A mousetrap is preferable to a cat any day in the week. Everyone knows that black cats are bad luck. I hope he won't come near me."

Mrs. Hankinson didn't get mad at all. She only smiled. "Oh, I don' think Jocelyn will. He ain't the sort to take up with folks who don' fancy cats." She turned to me. "You know, Amanda, Jocelyn ain't all black. If you look at his belly, you can see he's got a little bitty patch of white fur."

I watched Grandma stiffen even more. Oh, how she hated the word "belly." She was putting her back up all right, and she didn't take her eyes off the cat.

While the water boiled and Mrs. Hankinson made tea—real tea from India this time—I talked on and on about Edward T. Bone's being black as coal and how Allan would rig up a clothesline for her. All the time I was talking to Mrs. Hankinson I kept my eye on Grandma. I just knew she'd say something bad.

Finally she butted in. "I broke my hip four years back. Dr. Perkins says he never saw a person mend so fast. That's why I use a cane. I see you limp a little, Mrs. Hankinson?"

"Yes."

After she'd put the teacups on the table, Mrs. Hankinson went into the next room and came back with a shuttle and some tatting.

Mrs. Hankinson knew how to handle Grandma, who'd been trying to pry out of her what made her limp. "Yes" hadn't told her a danged thing.

Grandma changed her tack. "I see you like fancywork, Mrs. Hankinson. Do you crochet or knit too?"

Mrs. Hankinson nodded her head. "I do both of 'em." She smiled to herself, then added, "But they ain't what I really like to do."

"And what would that be? Embroidery?"

"Nope. What I like best is makin' quilts. That's why I fetched all this old cloth up here with me from Frisco. I guess you musta been wonderin' about the mess, huh?"

Quilts! Quilt making was what Grandma liked best, too.

Well, that solved the mystery of all the scraps of material and the queer washing.

Grandma leaned forward on her cane. "What kind of quilts? Pieced ones or laid-on ones?"

"All kinds of ones, Mrs. Barnett."

Grandma sat back. "I've made thirty-six of them. How many have you made?"

"Oh, dear, I lost count years ago—there's been so many."

This information didn't set well with Grandma. She put her jaw in a tight line and asked, "Would you show me some of them?"

"Be glad to." Mrs. Hankinson drank some tea, and then went into the next room. In a little while she returned with a quilt taken off her bed, probably. I liked it right away, because it was light blue and dark blue and white. I liked blue.

While I *oohed*, Grandma grabbed an edge of the quilt and turned it over to see how the corners had been sewed. She grunted, but still didn't say anything. I'd gone to the sewing circle a couple of times with her in Oysterville. Every time one of the old ladies sewed something that was so pretty all the others complimented her, my grandma had grunted like that.

"This pattern's the old Drunkard's Path, isn't it?" she asked Mrs. Hankinson. "Don't you think that's a wicked name for a pattern?"

Mrs. Hankinson smiled. "Well, I reckon that's one of the names for it. I call this quilt Wonder of the World. Other folks call it Fallin' Timbers."

"Or Fool's Puzzle," snapped Grandma Barnett, not to be outdone.

Mrs. Hankinson took the blue-and-white quilt back and brought out one that was orange, pink, light green, and peacock-feather blue. "This here's the old Basket of Tulips pattern," she told me.

"I made three of them for my relations," said Grandma, while she inspected the stitching. Then she let the quilt corner drop onto the floor, took up her teacup, and gulped down what was left of the scalding tea.

"Don't go, Mrs. Barnett. Let me show you the Colonial Rose I made last year."

"No." Grandma stood up. "I think Amanda and I should leave now. Thank you for the tea. We are having Reverend Pratt to supper." She nodded her head at Mrs. Hankinson, stumped off toward the door, jerked it open and went outside. We left so fast I didn't even hear Mrs. Hankinson say thank you for the jam and cake. As I helped Grandma up the sand dune, she muttered, under her breath, but I didn't catch one single word.

At the top I asked, "What'd you think of the new neighbor?"

"There's bad blood in that family all right! Mrs. Hankinson's vulgar—common and vulgar—if not downright morally bilious. She talked right out about 'bellies' and 'drunkards.' And Amanda, you told me yourself she sang yesterday about 'kissing' and loving somebody named George."

I couldn't help asking, "But what did you think of her quilts?"

"Passable—only passable."

"Are you going to ask her to the sewing circle meeting next Wednesday night?"

Grandma started home in a hurry. "Certainly not, girl. That woman would not fit in at all. So don't you say one word about her to the preacher tonight, or even again to me. She didn't even offer us a piece of your mother's cake, did you notice? That's just plain rude."

I hadn't thought it was, but in her mood there wasn't any use talking with Grandma. She was looking for a fight, and anybody she could beat would do. I followed along behind her in the ruts, wishing we hadn't ever gone to the silver shack.

Grandma clumped up onto the porch where Edward T. Bone was taking his ease in the afternoon sunshine. She jabbed him so hard with her cane he yelped, then got up and went down off the porch with his tail between his legs to hide in the snowball bushes.

"Confounded, worthless black dog—too lazy to scratch his own fleas or chase a no-good cat," Grandma said, and went inside.

I sat on the porch steps, getting madder by the second. She'd been horrible to Mrs. Hankinson for two reasons. Mrs. Hankinson was older than Grandma, and she was a better quilt maker. Grandma had liked being the oldest old lady on the Peninsula. And every year she entered a quilt in the Pacific County Fair and got the blue ribbon. Everybody said her stitches were the smallest they'd ever seen. I wasn't any real judge of quilt making, but Mrs. Hankinson's stitches had looked even smaller—close to invisible.

I got up after a while and went down on my hands and knees to coax Edward T. Bone out from under the snowball bush. "You can come out now," I whispered to him. "I think I have an idea how to make Grandma sorry she hurt you, Edward!"

MY IDEA WAS SO SINFUL I didn't lift my eyes off my plate at supper to look at Preacher Pratt or his wife.

As for John Pratt, when he said we ought to go out onto the front porch to look at the harvest moon, I said I'd rather look at "The Grandeur That Was Rome" on stereopticon slides with his mother. It would have been fun to hit him, though, when he tried to kiss me.

By now every girl in school had slapped him. Pheemie had even knocked him down when he smacked her. It wasn't that he was so awful because he liked kissing girls, but that he kissed everybody he could catch out of sight of her ma or pa or his. He wasn't one bit particular.

THE NEXT MORNING I was at school earlier than usual, busting with news. Molly, Jessy, Pheemie, and I formed a circle out in the schoolyard where Miss Coxe couldn't hear us. Then I told them all about Grandma and our going calling on Mrs. Hankinson.

"How awful that she didn't ask her into the sewing circle," said Molly.

"It was terrible of your grandmother to say what she did about Mrs. Hankinson's cat," Jessy told me.

Pheemie vowed, "I wouldn't treat a dog the way she treated Edward T. Bone. I hope she gets the spavins!"

I knew she wouldn't since that was a horse disease, but I was grateful all the same. "Well," I said, "she was even worse about the quilts, which were better than hers." Just then the school bell rang. I looked over my shoulder and saw Miss Coxe standing in the schoolhouse doorway, ringing her handbell, so I talked fast. "I think I know a way to put a spoke in my grandma's wheel!"

"What're you going to do, saw her old cane halfway through?" Jessy asked.

As we walked up to the schoolhouse, I told my friends what I had in mind. I felt sort of guilty about my plan, but Grandma had sure asked for it. I thought Molly would have been the first one to call me Benedict Arnold Barnett, but she didn't let out a peep about my being a traitor to my own flesh and blood.

All Molly said was, "We'll go call on Mrs. Hankinson this afternoon."

WE WERE AT THE DOOR of the silver shack at three-thirty on the dot. I was embarrassed to come calling three days in a row, but Mrs. Hankinson didn't seem fazed one bit. She said, "It's nice to see you again, girls," asked us in, and gave us more mint tea.

We'd decided on the way who was to be the spokesman. All of us wanted to be, but since the idea was mine they gave in. "We are a delegation," I started, "come to see your quilts. I saw them, but the rest of us didn't."

Mrs. Hankinson only smiled. She brought out one quilt after another. One of them, a patchwork, she called Martha

Washington's Flower Garden. She kept it on her lap while we talked, so I guessed it was her favorite. She pointed to a blue piece in it. "This came out of my husband's shirt, girls." She smiled as she put her finger on a piece of pink muslin. "This came out of my weddin' gown back home in Kentucky, and this white next to it is out of our oldest boy's christenin' dress." Then she touched a bright red piece and made a face. "This here's Turkey red cloth. I'm sick to death of it. Do you know it's the only red cotton we got in America that don' turn pink in three washin's?" She sighed. "Don' that beat all, though? We got only this Turkey red in a land as big and strong as ours. Mother Nature's got hundreds of reds. Take a look at a sunset or peony or geranium or apple. They're all different. But this old Turkey red is the only dye that's color-true in the country." Then she laughed. "I bet you can't guess what Turkey red's made out of, can you?"

I didn't know, and neither did anybody else.

"Hold your breath, girls. It's made out of ground-up beetle bugs from Mexico. Just think of that!"

I did, and the thought made me sick. Grandma Barnett used Turkey red all the time in her quilts, but I guess ground-up bugs wouldn't bother her.

Now that we'd had a look at some of her quilts, I jumped right in with my idea. "The County Fair is next September, and there's a prize for the best quilt."

"Is there, Amanda?" Mrs. Hankinson asked.

"There sure is, and we want you to win it," said Jessy.

"Amanda's grandmother is used to winning every

year, but we think you sew better than she does," said Pheemie.

"A whole lot better, Mrs. Hankinson," Molly added, leaning forward with her elbows on the table. "You have to make a brand-new quilt, though. It has to be sewed the year before the Fair. Have you got any ideas for a new one?"

Mrs. Hankinson started to count on her fingers, and I noticed how knotty and out of shape they were. "Well, I've done the Twinkling Star and Bridal Wreath, Tree of Life, True Lover's Knot, Christmas Star, and Indian Hatchet. And, oh yes, I forgot, that new pattern, Double Weddin' Ring."

"Which one of them do you want to make for the Fair?" asked Jessy.

"To tell the truth, girls, I'm pretty tired of all the ones I done before. I started sewin' when I was three years old. By the time I was seventeen and married, I'd already sewed thirteen quilts."

She patted Martha Washington's Flower Garden on her lap as if it had been her cat, closed her eyes, and then surprised us by starting to talk about something else entirely. "My husband was a singin' man back in Kentucky. He loved them old, old ballads that come over from England with our people before George Washington ever got born. My husband like to sing about red roses." When she opened her eyes, they were misty. "He always said the red rose was the only real rose. He didn' want no truck at all with yellow ones or pink ones. Sometimes he'd say that old poem aloud about a man's love bein' like a red, red rose.

And then he'd sing to me about the two doomed lovers, the fine lord and fair lady. Do you know about them two? There's somethin' about a red rose in that ballad."

I didn't, so I asked, "How were they doomed?"

"Feudin' families. Well, the lord and lady died of love and got buried side by side in the old graveyard."

I sure liked that. It made me feel sad and happy all at the same time. Then I remembered the name of one of the quilts she'd mentioned. "Mrs. Hankinson, why not do a True Lover's Knot?"

"No, Amanda. I done that one already. No, if I was goin' to make this quilt for a fair, it'd have to be a mighty special one—somethin' diff'runt from all the others. Let me do some thinkin' about it."

We were all quiet as mice in a sugar sack. After a little while she said, "I been thinkin' about a certain quilt ever since I was a bride sixty-three years back."

Jessy asked, "What's it called?"

"O the Red Rose Tree."

"There's an 'O' in it?" Pheemie was puzzled.

"Euphemia, if I say there's a 'O' in it, there is one. I'm makin' up the pattern, so it's mine to name."

I was excited. "Then it's a pattern nobody ever saw before. It'd be a brand-new quilt!"

Mrs. Hankinson nodded at me. "If it ever was to be, it would be somethin' new. But it's just a idea I had. I can't make it, girls."

"Why not?" asked Pheemie.

"Because it'll have seven roses—seven red ones, mostly all diff'runt shades of red. And not one of 'em that old

Turkey red. Those reds'll have to come from Europe. Foreigners got secret ways a dyein' cotton cloth." She nodded at us. "Oh, there'll be green leaves, lots of 'em. They'll be easy to find. But them reds that won' fade out in the wash would be troublesome." She shook her head so hard one of her tortoiseshell hairpins fell out of her bun onto the floor, startling Jocelyn. "Findin' seven reds I liked and had the money for has stopped me in my tracks for years, whenever I got the notion to make the quilt. I gave up lookin' for 'em.

"No, girls, that quilt's just another dream that can't never come true. Life's got a way of havin' quite a few of them kind of dreams. When I couldn' find the seven true-color reds I wanted and could afford to get, even down in Frisco stores that had bolts and bolts a cotton, I just give up. I found five of 'em there I fancied, but they cost too much money. That Europe-made cloth comes mighty dear."

"Do you remember your pattern for the quilt?" Molly aked her.

"Oh, girl, now would I forget that?"

"Then go ahead and make the quilt! Amanda and Jessy and Pheemie and I—we'll find the reds you need!"

I dropped my cup into my saucer. Molly had struck again! Impossible didn't mean a hoot or a holler to her. But why did she have to drag all of us in with her?

I waited for Mrs. Hankinson to say something like, "Thank you anyway, Molly, but I can't." Then I'd try to talk her into doing the Wreath of Roses patten because she liked roses so much. The quilt was on my bed right now. Grandma had given it to me on my eighth birthday. It had big pink roses with yellow centers and green leaves. But Mrs. Hankinson surprised me. What she said, smiling, was, "Thank you, Molly."

# 3

## The Impossible Begins

I WAS SO MAD at Molly Stevens that I wanted to shove my saucer in her mouth sideways, but it was too late.

Pheemie didn't help a bit. "Amanda's big brother can make a quilt frame for you, Mrs. Hankinson."

I didn't say a word. What was the use? All I could think of was where would we get seven different reds from Europe that wouldn't bleed. We lived in a place that had no cloth stores at all. Astoria, Oregon, across the Columbia River, was the closest place of any size, but it wasn't a real city. Portland was over a hundred miles from Astoria and the biggest city in our part of the world, but so far away I'd never even been there. Pa had. He said it was the "land of the nabobs," which was what he called rich swells.

I was feeling sour as all get-out when I felt Jessy pulling my arm out of its socket. "Hey, Amanda, what kind of quilt is your grandmother making this year?"

Telling that really would make me feel like Benedict Arnold, but I knew I had to tell or lie. Reluctantly I said, "It's the Woman's Christian Temperance Union pattern. It's green and white, the colors of the WCTU flag."

Pheemie scoffed. "O the Red Rose Tree ought to beat that all hollow. Green and white sounds dull to me."

I flared up. "Grandma knows her oats all right! The ladies who'll judge the quilts all belong to the WCTU, Pheemie. Anyhow, Grandma says it isn't so much the pattern that counts as the stitches."

We didn't stay much longer. I got everybody up and out by saying it was getting on toward sundown, and we all had chores to do at home. Up on top of the sand dune, though, I really tore into Molly Stevens. "Why'd you go and say we'd get the fancy red cloth she needs? How're we going to do that? We haven't got any money. Why don't you stuff your foot in your mouth *before* you open it—not afterwards?"

I put both ends of her long braids in her mouth. She got red in the face, but couldn't say anything. Oh, she knew I was right, and so did the others, now that they'd had some time to think about it.

"What're we going to do?" asked Pheemie.

"Talk her into pink roses or yellow ones or blue ones or Turkey red ones."

"There aren't any blue roses, Amanda," Pheemie explained. "She wants different colors of red ones. She won't ever stand still for Turkey red!"

"She's wanted them for sixty-three years!" Jessy said.

Molly spit out her braids. "Golly, Amanda, you're mean!"

"Rats! We're in a heckuva horrible mess," I said, and then tramped off home.

I'd go to Mrs. Hankinson's by myself the next day and

tell her Molly'd spoken too soon, and didn't she think pink roses would do just as well? I had a pink muslin dress I'd like to get rid of and find a home for in a quilt.

When I got back, Mama was sweeping off the sand that had blown onto the front porch that morning. She was frowning, so she didn't look half as pretty as she usually did. Mama was fair-haired and little. I resembled her. She looked up and sneezed. "Your grandmother's on another rampage, Amanda."

"What happened?"

"She had words with your father."

Well, that happened every so often. Mama thought they worked up to it for a while, and then both let fly. I guessed Pa had got the worst of it as usual and gone to the barn as he usually did. Mama said barns were "male refuges" in times of stress.

He was there, milking one of our Holsteins and chewing on his moustache. Pa was a big man like Allan, so big I could hardly see the stool he was sitting on. I stood in the empty cow stall next to him and leaned my elbows over the top. Milking was a pretty touchy business. If the milker got off his rhythm, he could annoy the cow and then she might not give as much milk. I didn't want to upset Pa any more than he was already, so I asked him, "Pa, what's your favorite color of rose?"

He didn't miss one squeeze in his milking. "Red, honey. None of the others I ever saw, even in Portland, the Rose City, can hold a candle to a deep, rich red rose. They smell best too."

That wasn't what I wanted to hear, but I thanked him

all the same and went to find my brother. Allan was forking hay into the team's mangers, working because Pa was there to watch him. He stopped when he saw me and leaned on the hayfork. "You're home pretty late, Amanda."

"I've been down to Mrs. Hankinson's again."

He nodded. "Next time you see her, tell her I'll be around pretty soon to rig up her clothesline. I guess it's the least the Barnetts can do for her after the way Grandma treated her."

"What'd Pa and Grandma fight about this time?"

"Grandma not asking Mrs. Hankinson to the church sewing circle. She bragged to him about it."

"Oh." Then I asked, "Allan, what's your favorite color rose?"

"Hmm." He leaned harder on the hayfork handle, looking off into the darkest corner of the barn. I thought he'd never get around to answering, but finally he said, "I think I favor those little climbing ones that Mrs. Stevens planted in front of the Life Saving Station. You know those red ones that look like burning coals in a fireplace."

Rats! I walked away. Men sure weren't a bit of help sometimes. I went to sit on top of a dune behind the barn to think. After a while I saw Dr. Alf's black buggy coming on the Nahcotta road. He was my last chance!

I ran down off the dune onto the road. Dr. Alf called out "Whoa" to Rosinante, so I didn't have to grab her bridle.

"What does the highwayman demand this time—my money or my life?" He was in a good mood.

"Is your patient getting well?"

"Uh-huh, and he paid me too. Out with it, Amanda."

I'd decided this time I would ask differently. "Dr. Alf, if you were going to send a lady a bunch of roses, what kind would you send?"

"Well, I'm certainly not about to, and I never have." He grinned. "But if I ever got the dangerous notion, I'd send American Beauties."

"What color are they?"

"Red—deep, rich red—like the heart of a ruby."

Rats, rats, and rats some more! Three out of three. Didn't men ever like any other kind? "Thank you for your opinion, Dr. Alf."

"It was nothing at all." He wasn't grinning as he leaned over the buggy seat. "Is something wrong? Maybe you need a tonic, Amanda. You look peaked."

I backed off fast. His tonics were brown and thick and came in heavy, brown bottles. "I feel just fine. It's only that Molly and Pheemie and Jessy and I are supposed to do something that's impossible."

"Humph! Well, as I always say, if it isn't injurious to the health of mind or body, attempting the impossible develops the character. Do it. Good-bye, Amanda. Giddap, Rosinante."

I wanted to sit right down in the ruts, but if Dr. Alf looked behind him and saw me, he'd think I was really sick when I was only sort of sick at heart. I went back toward the house, thinking. No, I wouldn't be able to talk Mrs. Hankinson out of red roses. She must want to make a quilt with them in because her husband, Lovin' George, had liked that kind of rose best, and it might be a way of remembering him. He'd even sung songs and recited poems about red roses. Men favored red roses all right. I guessed I'd better give in to them and to Mrs. Hankinson on this—not that I liked the idea.

MOLLY WAS WAITING for me on the road the next morning, looking mighty worried now that she'd had some time to think things over. And she was shivering, but that was because of the cold, not because she was scared of me. Oh, I'm fierce all right, but it doesn't last. I was shivering too. The ocean fog had been thick and cold last night. It was the kind of night when ships sometimes got wrecked and it gave us Peninsula folks the willies.

"Golly, Amanda," Molly called out to me. "I'm sure sorry I blurted some more."

I told her, "I forgive you, but I think maybe we shouldn't visit Mrs. Hankinson again till we've got something to show her. You made her a whopper of a promise. What she said about red is true. Mama told me last night that she knew of only two reds made out of cotton—that old Turkey red and red flannel. Red flannel bleeds so much when it's wet that ladies use it to color up their lips and cheeks. You know, Molly, getting seven different color-true reds isn't really possible, but I think we'll have to try anyhow."

Molly wailed, "But why can't we go down to the silver shack anymore?"

"Because Mrs. Hankinson might be sick of the sight of us by now."

Molly's face got long and sad. "She'll get lonesome."

"Oh, I'll talk to Mrs. Preacher Pratt about her next

Sunday. They'll call on her and invite her to church. Molly, we shouldn't get up Mrs. Hankinson's hopes too much about making O the Red Rose Tree." I had more to say, but it was almost time for school, so we ran along together in the sea mists that would blow away by noon.

Pheemie and Jessy were standing under a pine tree apart from the other kids, who were running around getting some of the hollering out of their systems before Miss Coxe rang the bell. Pheemie grabbed me by the jacket lapels. "Jessy's got a idea! It's about the quilt!"

Jessy looked as if she'd licked all the cream off her whiskers and liked the taste.

"Jessy, what is it?"

"Oh, Amanda, I know where there's a red we can use!"

"Where's that?" Molly asked.

"It's probably on Dr. Alf."

"*On* him!" I exploded.

Jessy jumped at me. "No, Amanda, it isn't his winter, red-flannel union suit, if that's what you're thinking! It's his chest protector, the one my mother made for him for Christmas two years ago for saving my brother Billy from the croup." She reached into her jacket pocket and brought out a little piece of red cotton cloth, not quite as bright as Turkey red. "This scrap was left over from the chest protector. I found it in Mama's sewing basket. I put it in a cup of water last night, and the water wasn't one bit red this morning, so it doesn't bleed."

"Where'd your ma get the cloth?" Molly asked.

Jessy shook her head. "I don't know." She stubbed the toe of her boot in the sand. "I think some relations back

East sent it to her, but I didn't ask because she'd want to know why I wanted to know. Amanda, I don't think we better tell anybody else on the Peninsula about what we're doing."

"Why not?" Grown-ups could be helpful sometimes. Miss Coxe might be. Schoolteachers were plenty smart about lots of things.

Jessy wouldn't look at me. "Because of *you*, Amanda! What'll people say if the word gets around that getting Mrs. Hankinson to make a quilt was your idea, and you're betraying your own grandmother?"

Pheemie giggled. "They'd probably say 'Hurray for Amanda.' "

"Lots of them would," Jessy agreed, "but some of the old ladies wouldn't. They'd tattle to old Mrs. Barnett right off." She glared at Pheemie. "Remember, Amanda has to live in the same house with her family."

I was so thunderstruck I didn't hear the schoolbell until Pheemie started hauling on me to get inside. Yes, Grandma Barnett would really skin my hide and nail it to the barn door if she found out I'd been the one to dream up Mrs. Hankinson's entering the quilt contest. And I wasn't at all sure Mama and Pa would approve. Allan might, though.

"What're we going to do—get Dr. Alf's chest protector?" I whispered to Pheemie, who sat in the school desk with me.

"Yep."

I whispered again, with one eye on Miss Coxe, who had the long wooden blackboard pointer in her hand. It was a fearful weapon. "How?"

"By almost dying off—one by one!" Then Pheemie stuck her nose into her McGuffey's Reader, and so did I.

But I couldn't keep my mind on the poem I was to recite that morning, "The Wreck of the Hesperus." Pheemie's answer was sure upsetting. I'd have worried more if she hadn't said "almost."

At recess I found out what Jessy's plan was. Her ideas were sort of wild at times, but this was the wildest one yet. Even Molly thought so. "Golly, Jessamine!" she exclaimed. "That's just awful. It could kill us!"

"No, we're going to get Dr. Alf the very minute we feel the symptoms coming on. He'll save us," said Jessy.

"But I don't want to get galloping pneumonia," I told Jessy. "Mama had it once and it nearly killed her."

She didn't even hear me, she was so fired up. "And when one of us gets to the pneumonia 'crisis,' she asks Dr. Alf on her deathbed to borrow his red chest protector to save her life. Doctors keep people's chests warm when they have pneumonia."

"How're we supposed to get pneumonia?" Molly was as leery of the scheme as I was.

Jessy's eyes were very bright. "There are lots of ways to catch colds. Colds are the beginnings of pneumonia."

Molly shook her head, hitting me in the face with her long braids. "Golly, Jessy, do we all have to get galloping pneumonia at the same time?"

Jessy was scornful. "No, just one at a time. I'm first. I'll give it two days, and then it's somebody else's turn for two days." She looked at me. "Amanda's next. We'll do it by the alphabet. Then comes Molly and then Pheemie." I didn't remind her that "Sharp" came before "Stevens" because she was already fishing in her pocket and bringing out three pieces of paper. She held them out like a fan. "Here, take one."

I asked. "What are they?"

"What each of you is supposed to do to get galloping pneumonia."

"Is it something different for each one of us?" squeaked Molly.

"It sure is. I thought hard about this!"

I sighed and took the middle slip. I read it and shuddered. "Mine's just awful! Jessy, what are *you* going to do? It better be as bad as mine."

"I soaked my petticoat in water and poured water all over my shoes before I started to school this morning. Didn't you hear me squishing when I went to the blackboard?"

True enough, Jessy had squished. "How do you feel?" I asked, hoping she felt something coming on already, so I wouldn't have to do what was written on my slip of paper.

"Just fine, Amanda, but if I don't catch a bad cold in two days, it's your turn." She looked fierce as could be. "We're keeping this secret from even Mrs. Hankinson."

"But, Jessy, what if Dr. Alf won't give us his chest protector?" I wanted to know.

"Oh, he will. He's a humanitarian." She scowled. "And if he doesn't, we'll tell everybody before we die that he refused out of the hardness of his cruel heart to humor a sick child."

At this point, Pheemie stuck in her oar. "What if one of

us gets galloping pneumonia and asks for the chest protector and he gives it to us, and then he wants it back after we don't die?"

Jessy shrugged. "That's easy. Remember, I've seen the chest protector. It's made in two layers. The red one is the top layer. The bottom's made out of white China silk, and we don't want that. We'll tell him we got mustard plaster on the white silk and ruined the whole thing." She paused and glared at each of us in turn, then lifted a finger in the air. "All right, now's the fatal hour." She crossed her heart. "Say after me, 'Cross my heart and hope to die if I don't do what I'm supposed to.' "

"Golly, Jessamine, couldn't you think of a happier way to get us to promise?" wailed Molly.

THE NEXT MORNING at school we felt Jessy's forehead to see if she was feverish. She wasn't, though she left wet tracks everywhere she walked. The plan wasn't working for her.

Next it was my turn. I thought my assignment was tougher than hers had been. I had to wait until everybody in my house had gone to bed, then go downstairs in my nightgown to the back porch, fill the chicken feed bucket with water from the kitchen pump, splash water all over my nightgown, open the back door, and sit in front of it with my feet in the bucket. The night wind off Willapa Bay was supposed to give me a cold for sure.

But I never caught anything at all! My forehead was cucumber-cool for two whole days.

On the third morning Jessy announced to Molly that it was her turn now.

For two nights Molly doused her head with water from the pitcher in her bedroom and went to bed with wringing-wet hair that soaked her pillow. We believed her because her braids were still damp in the mornings when we felt her cool forehead.

"Euphemia, you're our last chance!" Jessy declared finally. "You must swim tomorrow!"

I was sorry for Pheemie. It was a horrible day, very close to Halloween, and raining hard. I asked Jessy, "Wouldn't standing out in the rain at midnight in her nightgown be enough?"

"Nope," said Jessy. "It's against the rules."

"I'll do it," Pheemie told us grimly, "but somebody has to go with me. Mama won't let me take the crab rake out alone."

We all knew how darned dangerous crab holes were. They could look shallow, but be very deep. One end of a crab hole was almost always out in the surf where sometimes there was quicksand. People got drowned in them all the time.

I said, "Allan'll go. And so can I if he does."

Pheemie blushed. "Amanda, I was going in my union suit—not all my clothes."

"It doesn't matter how you go, Pheemie," said Jessy. "Just fall in—clothes and all."

"But, Amanda, what if I fall in two afternoons in a row like I have to and I don't catch cold, won't that look queer to your brother? If he thinks I'm so dumb, he'll never ask me to dance at the square dances."

That was the first time I knew Pheemie had her eye on Allan, too. I said, "Don't worry about him. He never dances with a girl who doesn't ask *him*. Allan doesn't do the asking."

Allan went crabbing two days with us while Pheemie fell in twice. The first time she splashed in and floundered across a crab hole, but some big waves carried her into deep water, and Allan had to wade out and pull her from the ocean. The next time wasn't so dangerous. When she fell in, I stuck out the handle of the crab rake and let her pull herself ashore.

Although we got two crabs each time, she didn't catch cold. It was very discouraging.

We'd failed. We'd kept away from Mrs. Hankinson while we tried to get galloping pneumonia and the chest protector. Now we'd have to go to her empty-handed. We couldn't put off calling on her forever, and we figured she might be lonesome. So we started out together one day after school, walking in the ruts, feeling down-at-the-mouth but healthy.

On the way north out of Nahcotta we ran into Dr. Alf, going south.

"Aha! He of the red chest protector!" hissed Jessy to me.

She stepped back off the road so he could pass, but I grabbed Rosinante's bridle, because I had a medical question to ask him. "Has anybody ever tried to get a cold and got one?"

"Not that I ever heard of. I tried it myself once in medical school to get out of an examination. Sat in a Vermont ice house all night and never ran one degree of fever afterwards."

"Ah," we said all together like choir singers.

The doctor looked puzzled, then hauled out his big gold watch. "I have to be getting on now, girls." He smiled down at me. "Amanda, I met your Mrs. Hankinson the other day. She sent for me."

"Golly, is she sick?" asked Molly.

"Not too bad off. She sent for me in time."

"What's she got?"

"Congestion of the lungs. It could easily have turned into galloping pneumonia, though, at her age. She'll be all right if she stays in bed and keeps warm."

We looked at each other, our mouths hanging open. Of course, Dr. Alf didn't understand why. He thought we were worried about Mrs. Hankinson. "You can go see her if you don't stay too long," he said. "Take her some clam broth maybe tomorrow. I carted a load of supplies into that shack of hers so she won't starve. Don't get upset about her. She's all right for now. I gave her my chest protector to wear."

*"Your red chest protector?"* Jessy almost shouted.

Dr. Alf put his finger to his lips. "Don't tell your mother, Jessamine. It was so small it covered only my left lung. Everytime I wore it I could hardly move. Mrs. Hankinson's so little it fits her fine. I'm glad somebody can get some good out of it."

Jessy was beaming. "I won't tell Mama. I promise."

"We all promise," said Pheemie. And we all crossed our hearts again.

I could hardly believe what had happened. At the top of Mrs. Hankinson's sand dune I told the others what Dr. Alf had said about the "impossible" developing character when it didn't injure the body or mind.

"He's absolutely right," Jessy declared. "Doing what we did stiffened our backbone a lot." Then she slid down the dune on part of her stiffened backbone. So did the rest of us.

Mrs. Hankinson would never know how we'd failed at getting her the first red for O the Red Rose Tree. But it didn't matter. We still had six reds to go, and my soul wasn't filled with a lot of hope. If those reds weren't easier to come by than the first one, I was pretty sure we wouldn't survive till summer.

THE SUNDAY AFTER we'd visited Mrs. Hankinson and admired her new red chest protector every one of us caught a cold in Oysterville—at church. Preacher Pratt, his wife, and John all had colds. Kissin' John gave Molly a big smack behind her pa's buggy before Sunday school. He got Pheemie in the church vestibule while she was ringing the church bell. She knocked him down, but it was too late. She'd been kissed! John grabbed me and kissed me when we had to go inside a dark closet together to get more hymn books for some people visiting from South Bend. I hit him on the head with a hymnal—too late. Jessy got smacked behind the church when she went to get her little brothers off the rope swing the Sunday-school teacher had made. She said she bit and kicked him.

All of us stayed home from school Monday through Friday because of our colds. Grandma Barnett scared Mama half out of her wits by saying I was on the verge of galloping pneumonia and that I could have a crisis at any moment. But we didn't even have to call in Dr. Alf. I just blew my nose for five days straight and got it all red.

Rats!

# 4

*Flotsam*

Mrs. Hankinson got better after Halloween, but she still coughed some, I noticed. When she was up and around, we called on her in another delegation to tell her about the chest protector being color-true. She brought it out of her bedroom and held it up. "Hmmm, the top layer is cotton, ain't it? I guess I felt too poorly to take notice. It won' bleed, you say?"

"No, ma'am," Jessy assured her.

"Do you think there's enough cloth in it for a rose?" asked Molly, before Mrs. Hankinson could ask Jessy how she knew it wouldn't bleed.

"No," Mrs. Hankinson said, "but it'll make a fine, handsome rosebud."

I was hoping our getting the chest protector left only six reds to go. Were there going to be buds, which meant more cloth? "A bud?" I asked.

"Two buds, Amanda. And five big roses—all different shades of red, of course."

I heaved a sigh of relief. Still only six to go, but I supposed she needed really good-sized pieces of red cloth for the blooming flowers. I'd never realized before just how enormous a quilt was!

"What about the green leaves and the rest of the cloth?" Pheemie wanted to know.

"They'll have to be got at a store, Euphemia."

This information made us look at our boots. Even in good times money was scarce on the Peninsula. But the times weren't good. It was 1893 and the whole country was "suffering," according to what President Cleveland said in the Astoria newspapers we sometimes saw. Not that we Peninsula people were starving. As long as there were oysters and fish in Willapa Bay and clams and crabs on the beach, the supper table was set. The ocean was a good provider. But that still didn't mean we had cash.

"We haven't got any money," said Jessy finally.

"But I have!" exclaimed Mrs. Hankinson. "I have some money I was saving for a rainy Monday—a whole quarter eagle. I think I'd rather use it for the quilt than a rainy Monday."

Two dollars and fifty cents in gold! Mrs. Hankinson got up and took a tiny little gold piece out of her tea canister. She held it between two fingers. "Who'll go to a store and buy what I'm goin' to need for O the Red Rose Tree?"

Jessy, whose Pa ran a general store in Nahcotta, told her, "The nearest store that'd have a lot of cloth is in Astoria."

"Uh-huh, C.H. Cooper's Dry Goods," I put in. Now I thought hard. Allan had said he was going to Astoria "pretty soon." If Grandma Barnett, who liked gadding around, didn't go with him, I would. "My big brother's going to Astoria pretty soon, I think," I told Mrs. Hankinson.

"Oh, he's a fine young fellow, reminds me of my husband," said the old lady. By now we figured her husband had been "Lovin' George" and he was the real reason she wanted to make O the Red Rose Tree, though he'd been dead a long, long time. That was sure romantic! She went on talking about Allan. "He fixed me up a good clothesline, and he's fetched me a lot of clams and fish lately."

"He *has*?" I was surprised. Allan hadn't told me.

"Yes. Tell your mother for me I think he's a pure treasure. You certainly come from nice folks, Amanda."

I couldn't say anything but "thank you," because I was thinking of Grandma Barnett's behavior. I knew that to keep the peace in our house Mama hadn't dared come calling at the silver shack.

"Why don't you make a list of what you're going to need?" I asked, as Jocelyn jumped up on my lap, dug his claws into my knees to get comfortable, and settled down. He was a real hefty cat.

While she was gone in her little bedroom, Jessy hissed at me, "Do you think you can do this all alone, Amanda?"

I hissed back, "Well, you can come along if you want. It's a big responsibility!"

Mrs. Hankinson returned with a scrap of paper and a pencil stub. I noticed how she wrote, not good at all. She wasn't a good speller, and her fingers were stiff, but she got the words down somehow. Then she read out loud, "A big white sheet, cotton quilt batting, four yards a white muslin for the blocks, three yards a green for regular leaves, two yards of another green for new leaves, one yard for little old leaves, good strong cotton thread in green to match the leaves, lots a white thread to do the quiltin'."

All that stuff was going to be heavy. I guessed I was going to be a beast of burden and also be responsible for getting the right greens. "Have you got the pattern all figured out?" I asked Mrs. Hankinson, hoping she wasn't ready.

"Oh, yes, dear." She reached inside a drawer under the table and pulled out a drawing made in pencil. The roses weren't the ordinary round, flat open ones ladies usually sewed in a quilt block. They were "laid on," appliquéd, and the leaf patterns had real jaggedy points at the ends. I'd never before seen a quilt pattern like that.

"My gosh!" said Pheemie, Molly, and Jessy together. I didn't say anything.

THE WEEK BEFORE Thanksgiving, Allan and I went to Nahcotta and got on the train that ran twenty miles south to Ilwaco. Lucky for us, Grandma Barnett had decided that November's "foul weather" made the Columbia River we had to cross rough enough for her to get seasick.

As we sat across from each other on the red plush train seats, I asked Allan, "Will you keep a secret?"

"Sure, if you'll keep one." Allan was the most agreeable person I'd ever met. "You tell me your secret first."

I knew I'd have to confide in him so he could help me carry all that cloth in Astoria and get it back home. I was a little bit scared, though, at what he'd think when he found out I was betraying Grandma by helping Mrs. Hankinson.

He listened, then laughed after the engineer tooted the train whistle to tell Ilwaco the train was coming. "That's some secret, Amanda. It'll do Grandma good to miss out on one blue ribbon in her life. Do you think Mrs. Hankinson can get the quilt done in time? She seems pretty feeble to me."

"Oh, she can do it, but I don't think we can get those reds in time. If she couldn't find them in sixty-three years, how can we in less than a year?"

"There are four of you! If I was betting, I'd bet you kids do it."

I didn't agree, so I changed the subject. "Allan, what's your secret?"

"I'm looking for a berth on a ship bound out of Astoria—the South Seas maybe."

"Oh, Allan!" I put my hand over my mouth. He'd fibbed to Pa and to Mama too. He'd told them he had friends to see in Astoria about work in a lumber mill. I'd said I was going to do some Christmas shopping for Mama, and I was, but only for some gift makings that she needed. "Why're you going away? Is it because Grandma Barnett's so terrible?"

He shrugged. "That's part of it. There's nothing much to keep me on the Peninsula anyway."

"There's the Life Saving Service at Klipsan Beach or Fort Canby. You could join it."

He made a face. "No, that's only a couple of miles from home. I'm getting restless. I want to see something of the world before I settle down. If I find a ship today, I'll come home with you and tell everybody good-bye and pack what things I'll need."

I was worried so much about Allan that I didn't get sick on the boat crossing the Columbia, even though the wide river was dark gray with white-cap waves. Cold rain kept spitting in my face under my sou'wester as I stood at the rail watching Astoria, Oregon, get closer. Astoria was always exciting, with lots of ships anchored in the river and at the docks, taking on cargoes of canned fish and lumber. The lower part of town, Astor Street, was pretty rough, so Allan squired me from the steamer wharf where we landed up to the dry-goods store on Commercial Street. Then he left for Astor Street, promising to meet me at three o'clock at Colman's Ice Cream Parlor.

C.H. Cooper's Dry Goods nearly drove me out of my mind! I saw only Turkey red cotton, but there must have been ten different green cottons. Willow green, serpent green, crystal green, forest green! I wanted to howl and bellow. What were rose-leaf greens?

A man clerk came up to me while I was dripping rain off my sou'wester brim onto the cloth. "Look out there, little lady," he said. "You're getting the merchandise wet. Can I help you?"

He didn't look to me as if he knew anything much about rose colors either. "Have you got a lady clerk?"

He grinned. I guess he thought I wanted to buy corset covers or "unmentionables." I was embarrassed, so I gave him my fiercest look, which made him go away. In a minute a big lady with a high blond pompadour came out of the back of the store. From Mrs. Hankinson's list I read off: the sheet, batting, muslin, and white thread. Then I asked, "Do you grow roses?"

She blinked. "Roses? Well, yes. I have a couple of bushes."

I decided I'd have to let her in on our secret. "I'm making a quilt that has roses and leaves, and I need green cloth."

She smiled. "Well, you certainly ought to be able to find a suitable green here."

"I need three kinds."

"Three?" Her eyebrows lifted. "That's a lot of greens for one quilt if they're supposed to be only rose leaves."

"They have to be just right. They have to be old and new and regular leaves."

"Well, let's see." She walked over to a bolt of bright green cloth. "This is the color of new leaves." Then she showed me another bolt, a darker green. "How does this look to you for the regular, mature leaves?"

"All right, I guess, if you say so." But nothing I saw looked right to me for the old leaves on O the Red Rose Tree.

Finally the lady clerk crooked a finger for me to follow her to the other end of the store. From behind a counter she brought out a green that looked as if it had bronze metal in it. "How much do you need, little girl?" she asked.

"This is the identical green of the oldest leaves on my rose bushes."

"One yard, and green thread to match all the greens."

As she cut and folded the cloth, the way she had the other pieces, she told me, "You may wonder why this particular green wasn't out with the others. I'll tell you a secret. The mayor's youngest daughter might be an elf in her school Christmas pageant, and her costume will be made out of this. She won't need all the cloth, so I gave you some, seeing as how you live across the river. What are you going to be at Christmas?"

"Tired!" I answered, thinking of the awful work ahead, getting six more reds for the quilt. Then, because she'd been so nice to me, I asked her, "What are the reds in cotton made of except for ground-up Mexican beetles?"

"You must be referring to Turkey red." She knew her oats all right. "Well, there's another red that's color-true. It's made out of madder root in Europe, but I haven't any of that here now. And then there are those lovely but expensive reds the Germans make. They have a secret way of dyeing that nobody else in the world knows. The color-true reds that aren't made from beetles or madder root come from Germany."

I thanked her and left the store for Colman's, lugging the big package. I was mighty glad to unload it onto Allan while I carried the little package of ribbon, lace and ecru tatting thread I'd promised to get for Mama.

"Did you find a ship?" I asked Allan over peppermint-stick ice cream at the parlor.

"No. None of them are going any place I want to go."

Afterward we headed back to the steamer and got aboard. This time we stayed belowdecks in the tiny oil-stinking cabin, sitting across from a Chinese man in a long black overcoat and derby hat. He noticed the big brown-paper-wrapped bundle beside me, and asked, "You got laundry there, little Missy?"

I laughed. I guessed the package did look like ironed laundry. Chinese ran laundries in lots of places, but the men on the Peninsula worked in the cranberry bogs. Pa said they never bothered anybody and were good workers who kept to themselves. I was a little bit scared of them, though, because Grandma had told me some were criminals—highbinders.

"No, it's cloth for a quilt," I told him, hoping he wasn't a hatchet-throwing highbinder.

"Are you from Ilwaco?" Allan asked him.

"I Lee Bing Hung." He smiled. "I come from Portland. I do laundry there, but get tired of big flatiron. Now I come to work with cousins in Ilwaco. Who you be, please?"

Allan introduced both of us, then went over to sit next to the young man. By the time we got to the Washington side of the Columbia, they seemed to know each other pretty well. Allan told me when we got off the steamer that Lee had been educated in mission schools in Portland's Chinatown and was very ambitious to be "somebody big" someday. He wasn't a highbinder at all.

"How's he ever going to be somebody big if he picks cranberries up here?" I asked Allan.

"He doesn't plan to do that all his life." Allan helped me onto the train and sat next to me, frowning. "Pa told me once that the boss of the Chinese workers in Ilwaco is a pretty mean cuss. I've seen him. He looks it."

Well, I wasn't too worried about a stranger like Lee Bing Hung the way I was about the quilt. I asked Allan, "Will you take the bundle to Mrs. Hankinson for me? It's pretty heavy."

"Sure, honey."

I reached into my oilskins' pocket and gave him six cents. "This is her change. Please stay at the silver shack long enough to find out if she likes the three greens I bought."

I WAS HOME an hour before Allan. He'd been gone so long Grandma was annoyed. "Where have you been?" she snapped at him as he took off his oilskins on the back porch.

"Courtin'," he told her. "Courtin' a lovely lady down by Nahcotta."

I wanted to giggle, but didn't dare. I guessed he meant Mrs. Hankinson, although maybe he'd stopped off someplace else along the road home. There wasn't a girl on the Peninsula who wouldn't swoon away if he dropped in.

Disgusted, Grandma snorted so loud she woke up Edward T. Bone from his sleeping place. I waited till she was gone to ask, "What did she say about the greens?"

"She said she couldn't have done better herself. She's starting in on the quilt right away and says to tell you thank you and that you're the most rugged child she's ever known!"

*Child! Rugged!* Those awful words were my thanks for all the shopping I'd done and for trying to almost die of pneumonia. Grown-ups sure were queer sometimes, even the nicest ones like Mrs. Hankinson.

\* \* \*

ALLAN SHOT FOUR DUCKS on Willapa Bay two days before Thanksgiving. Three were for our holiday dinner, and the other was for Mrs. Hankinson. I took the duck to her in a gunnysack on my way to school the same morning Allan shot it, and told her, "Before you eat it, be sure you get all the birdshot out, or it'll bust your teeth."

"I know, dear. Thank you," she said, taking the sack.

"How's the quilt coming, Mrs. Hankinson?"

"Just fine, except for the rest of the reds."

I sighed. "Well, couldn't there be pink roses in it, too, along with the red bud from the chest protector?"

"Now, Amanda." She put her head to one side, smiling. "Did you ever see a red bud on a pink rosebush?" When I didn't answer, she asked, "What are you making your family for Christmas?"

"A yellow silk hair-receiver bag for Mama to put her hair combings in."

"That has to be sewed, don' it, and well sewed, too? Why don' you ask Jessy and the others to come here Saturday afternoons, and I'll help you out with your sewin'?" She stooped to stroke Jocelyn, who'd come to the door. "That way I can pay you back a bit for all you're doin' for me."

I thought that was a good idea and so did the others, so we showed up sharp at one o'clock Saturday with our work baskets. Molly was knitting navy blue wristlets for her father and little brothers. Pheemie was crocheting a purple silk holder for a ball of twine for her mother and making a gilded horseshoe pasted on a red satin background picture frame for her pa. Jessy had something different. She brought along a wire broiler, some blue plush, and gold paint to make a newspaper holder for her father. I was making the hair receiver for Mama, whiskbroom holders out of black velveteen for Pa and Allan, and a petal-shaped, lavender pincushion for Grandma.

Mrs. Hankinson helped us more than she worked herself on O the Red Rose Tree, though I could see that she had cut out cardboard pieces to outline the patterns and piled them up on top of a box.

While Jessy was working away on the wire broiler and Pheemie was painting her horseshoe gold, Mrs. Hankinson helped Molly untangle her wristlet yarn, then showed me how to take tinier stitches.

Finally she coughed, and said, "Amanda, I sewed better'n you when I was five years old. Your stitchin' goes every which way. Because of that your fancywork's cattywampus."

I got mad. Pheemie sewed worse than I did. That's why she pasted horseshoe picture frames. Molly was a terrible knitter. I said, "Molly knits bad, but not as bad as she sews! Everytime Jessy picks up a needle, she stabs herself with it, and Pheemie'd rather paste than sew!"

My friends were glaring at me. "Golly, Amanda, you're sure *mean*," said Molly.

"Rats!" I threw down the hair receiver.

"There, there, Amanda," Mrs. Hankinson said, trying to pour oil on my troubled waters. "I'll teach all of you girls how to sew. You'll sew better in no time." She picked up the hair receiver and went to the window, where she could see better, to pull out my stitches.

Molly whispered, "Amanda, your own grandma kept Mrs. Hankinson out of the church sewing circle. My mother says Preacher Pratt's wife is too scared of your grandmother to dare ask her into it. Mama says elderly ladies need sewing circles. Mrs. Hankinson hasn't got one, so here's our chance to be it!"

I chewed that over for a while. I wasn't crazy about sewing or any other kind of fancywork. Grandma Barnett had tried to teach me, but she yelled so much when I made a mistake that she gave me the willies and I quit. "Oh, all right," I told them all, as I took back the hair receiver and started in again.

"Maybe someday we'll be quilt makers, too!" said Jessy, when Mrs. Hankinson got up later on to make us mint tea. "Amanda, how's your grandmother coming along with her quilt?"

"She's piecing it now. It's going along pretty fast." I didn't tell them I thought the blocks were handsome. They were a couple of greens, but not the same colors I'd bought in Astoria. Grandma had been saving green scraps for a long time for this WCTU quilt.

"Golly, we'd better get going to find those six other reds," said Pheemie.

I was sarcastic. "Oh, sure. Pray for a miracle."

"I am praying every single night for one," exclaimed Jessy. "The Lord will provide again—like he provided the chest protector!"

"Jessamine, I go along with what my pa says," I told her. " 'The Lord helps those that help themselves.' "

"Oh, grown-ups are great on sayings," said Pheemie.

"My mother always says, 'The Lord works in mysterious ways His wonders to perform.'"

"I believe that one too!" cried Jessy.

I had my finger in my mouth, because I'd just drawn blood with my needle. Otherwise, I would have said what I thought about those sayings of theirs.

THE FIRST WEEK of December was just terrible. The weather turned so bad we could hardly make it to school because of the wind and the water in the road. The hens stayed in the hen house all day. The sand blew so hard that Pa kept off the roads with the team, and Edward T. Bone wouldn't budge from under the kitchen stove. Our house rattled and shook in the wind that came roaring over the sand dunes from the sea. Everybody got nervous, even Horace, who cried day and night. When Mama wasn't walking him, Allan was. Grandma Barnett was more snappish than ever and quicker to give orders.

The fourth night of the storm Mama said at supper, "I pity all poor sailors at sea."

Grandma humphed at her. "They don't deserve it, Adelaide. They're danged fools to go to sea in the first place."

I stole a glance at Allan, hoping he'd pay heed and give up looking for ships, and just as I looked away from him, we heard the sound. It was a new one—a dull boom— over the pounding and rattling of the gale. Startled, Pa and Allan looked up from their plates, then at each other. They got up, threw down their napkins, and headed for the back porch. Mama's face had drawn tight, as mine must have too. We knew what that boom was. A ship's cannon, the signal for a ship in distress.

Dressed in their black oilskins and carrying ropes, Pa and Allan headed west across the dunes, as we knew other Peninsula men were doing. They'd try to help the Life Saving Service if they could.

Mama and I cleared the table and put the dishes on to boil without saying a word to each other. Finally I said, "Mama, because tomorrow's Saturday, and if the ship doesn't founder and any drowned men get washed up onto the sand, can I go to the beach if the storm's over?"

"That's a large number of 'ifs,' Amanda."

"But I want to see what gets washed overboard off the ship!" I loved the beach the day after a storm even better than an eerie walk.

Mama said, " 'Flotsam' is the word for what gets washed overboard. All right, if the storm's over and the ship hasn't gone down and all the sailors are safely ashore, you may go."

"May I sit up for Pa and Allan tonight?"

"Yes—until midnight." Mama listened for a minute, then let out a deep sigh. Horace was yelling again. I guessed she'd be up till all hours too. Grandma would go to bed at nine-thirty, as always, on the bong of our grandfather's clock.

OUR MEN WERE BACK at eleven-thirty, wet and tired. Over hot coffee, which Mama made for them, Pa told us about the bark. She was wrecked—the *Geoffrey Barr* out of Liverpool bound for Vancouver, British Columbia. The Klipsan Beach Life Saving Station had done their work well and got all the crew and the captain off. The bark, her rigging destroyed, was offshore, listing hard to port in the surf, but not so much that she'd heel over and lose all her cargo. The salvage companies would retrieve most of it.

"What was the cargo?" Mama wanted to know.

"The ship's captain said the cargo's just about everything that's made in England—chinaware, knives and cutlery, cloth, but mostly gin."

"Cloth?" I exploded.

Pa looked surprised. "Sure, Amanda, cotton and wool cloth from English mills."

"Is the storm stopping, Pa?"

"It looks to be."

I figured the storm was slowing down a half hour before they got home, when our house stopped banging around so much.

Well, now I knew I'd be up at dawn and probably so would Molly. Her pa, being the officer in charge of the Life Saving Station, would tell her about the cargo of the *Geoffrey Barr*. She'd be beachcombing, too, if she wasn't already out with a lantern.

MAMA LET ME LEAVE at six o'clock. The morning was cold as heck but so sunshine-bright that my eyes watered. I covered the mile over the plank road laid on top of the sand as fast as I could and ran down onto the ocean beach.

Though the surf was rough and high because of last night's storm, the water was blue as could be.

The beach was an exciting mess that morning and already full of Peninsula folks poking around in the brown kelp that had torn loose from the ocean bottom. They were looking for flotsam from the *Geoffrey Barr*. I got myself a long driftwood stick and poked here and there in the brown seaweed, lifting up long trailing bits, but I found nothing except dead crabs and pieces of old wood.

Then I heard somebody yelling my name, and there was Molly running toward me.

"The ship was carrying cloth from England!" she cried.

"Oh, I know that," I told her sourly, "but no cloth got washed ashore. If it did, somebody else grabbed it first."

"Would red *English* cotton turn pink, too, Amanda?"

"Gosh, Molly, I don't know. All I know is that English cotton isn't made in America. Maybe English cotton is dyed with that secret stuff from Germany."

"Golly, Amanda, I hope so."

Molly and I hunted and hunted. We even waded out in our gum boots near the wrecked *Geoffrey Barr*, but we found nothing worth taking home. Finally Molly said glumly, "Well, come on home with me. Mama'll make us hot cakes. She likes you, Amanda, even if she can't stand your grandmother."

Hot cakes sounded like a good idea, and I could do with a second breakfast. Flotsam had failed us. We turned south and walked on the hard, smooth wet sand for a long time. We passed quite a few other disappointed beachcombers when we saw a man walking toward us, wearing a long black overcoat and a derby hat. On top of his overcoat was something darkish red, a long wide strip hanging down from around his neck like a muffler.

"Hey, I know him. That's Lee Bing Hung," I told Molly.

"Who's he?"

"A Chinese man from Ilwaco. Don't be scared of him."

As we came up to him, he tipped his derby to me and grinned. "Hello some more, Missy Barnett."

"Hello, Lee Bing Hung." I was staring at the red muffler, which wasn't a muffler at all. It was cloth, torn in quite a few places, and it was sure red! "Where'd you find that old red rag?" I'd heard the Chinese were good traders, and I was being clever.

He pointed to the ocean. "Lee leave cranberry bogs and bad Boss for while. Lee go walking and find beautiful, fine red cloth on the beach."

I circled him, staring at the cloth. "It came off the wrecked ship, huh?"

He only smiled.

I whispered into Molly's ear, "We have to get that cloth!" Then I asked Lee Bing Hung, "What'll you take for that dirty old shipwreck rag?"

"What will Missy Barnett give Lee for it?"

Rats! I didn't have anything at all on me but a pocket comb with two teeth missing and a harmonica I'd won in a marbles game at school. I fished out the harmonica. "How about this?"

He took it, pocketed it right off, then said, "What else you give for fine red cloth?"

I was about to offer the comb, but Molly asked him, "What do you want?" She was some trader!

His answer jolted us both. "Spuds! Want four great big spud potatoes. Lee like spuds!"

"Heck, I'll give those to you," promised Molly. "My mother's got lots of them. Come back to the Life Saving Station with me and get them."

"Will do. Deal made." Lee Bing Hung removed the red cloth from around his neck and gave it to Molly. Though it was full of holes, there were some good solid spots left in it. The cloth must have caught on something in the wreck and got torn before the waves got it.

Molly and I ran out together into the surf and dipped one end of the cloth into the salt water. We squeezed it into the palm of her hand, holding our breath. Not even one pink drop of water fell on her palm. The cloth didn't run! Glory be!

"You take it to Mrs. Hankinson, Amanda, while I pry four big potatoes out of Mama," Molly told me.

By law the cloth was ours. Flotsam belonged to anybody who got it. "What'll I tell Mrs. Hankinson, Molly?"

"Tell her to wash it good in fresh water and iron it." She laughed at me. "Jessy's right. The Lord is providing, Amanda."

I didn't laugh. I was sort of scared.

While I folded the cloth, Lee Bing Hung asked, "Why you want old shipwreck rag, Missy Barnett? You crazy?"

"I wouldn't be a bit surprised," I told him.

# 5

# *Maud Williams*

We kept on working on our Christmas presents Saturdays at Mrs. Hankinson's, tearing out stitches and untangling yarn, while she sewed on the quilt blocks for O the Red Rose Tree. She was coming along with the green leaves and one rosebud block, but I wasn't doing so well on Mama's hair receiver. I had to pull the stitches out so often the silk was getting torn.

"You'll have to get more silk and start all over, Amanda," Mrs. Hankinson told me finally. "I hope you won't have to go all the way to Astoria for it."

I hoped so too.

"Oh, she won't," said Jessy. "Our store's got a quarter yard of pink satin left over from a petticoat my mother made." At Jessy's folks' store you could buy everything from gumdrops to horse collars, but only calico and flannel. Oysterville's two stores were like the Reeds' store—not much cloth either.

I made a face. "I hate pink. Mama hates it too."

"Well, then, we'll go to Ilwaco on the train. Maybe we'll

find something there that's a color you fussy Barnetts can stand," snapped Jessy.

"We?" I asked her. "What do you have to do in Ilwaco?"

"Look for toys for my brothers and little sister. You don't expect me to give them stuff out of our own store that they've seen all year, do you? We'll go next Saturday morning."

I dropped the yellow hair receiver and started to daub Grandma's pincushion with flour paste to glue on the felt flower petals. Doing that made me think of sticking pins into it, which led me to thinking of Grandma. She was getting worse, complaining all the time. I'd noticed Allan had quit sweet-talking her, and he and Pa spent lots of time out in the barn, leaving Mama and me for her to jump on all the more. That wasn't fair at all—the more people around, the less any one person had to suffer.

Grandma had ripped into me that morning because I kept going down to that "morally bilious" Mrs. Hankinson's. She said the four of us girls shouldn't go pestering that "poor old lady" so much. Elderly women didn't like "girl gigglers" around; they liked "peace and quiet" in their lives. I'd got over feeling guilty about helping Mrs. Hankinson compete with Grandmother at the County Fair. I wanted to be there wearing my best bonnet to see the blue ribbon on Mrs. Hankinson's red rose quilt.

THE NEXT SATURDAY MORNING Jessy and I climbed onto the train and went to Ilwaco. We got mechanical iron banks for her brothers, a spinning top for her sister, and a half yard of black taffeta for Mama's new hair receiver. Black wouldn't show the stitches so much. I was sick of sewing. Jessy didn't think she'd ever be a good seamstress either.

As we got back on the train for Nahcotta, she started to tell me how fumble-thumbed Pheemie and Molly were, too, when a lady came down the aisle and sat down across from us. In her arms was a baby all wrapped up in a blue blanket.

We stared at this stranger. She had red hair coiled up in a twisty bun behind her head, and it curled around her freckled face in the front. Her eyes were pale blue-green and slanted up at the corners. She had on a plain dark blue Newmarket coat with brass buttons and a black hat with a big red ribbon on it. I guessed she must have been about twenty-one, not young but not so old either. She smiled at us and jiggled the baby in her arms.

I knew a lot about babies because of Horace. He would have yelled plenty if I'd jiggled him like that. "What's the baby's name?" I asked the lady.

She wrinkled up her forehead as if she couldn't remember what it was, then said, "Oh, I call her Ebenezer."

"Ebenezer!" Jessy said. We looked at each other. The lady had said *her*!

"Ebenezer's sure a quiet baby," I said, as the train started off with a big jolt and I jerked backward, snapping my neck.

"Yes, he hasn't let out a peep since we left Missouri ten days ago."

Jessy and I looked at each other again. Now the baby was a *he*!

"Is the baby your baby?" asked Jessy.

The lady chuckled. "Of course it is. I got it in Saint Louis."

*It?* Golly, I'd wanted to see the baby when she first got on, but now I decided not to talk about it anymore. So I asked, "Do you have relations here on the Peninsula, Mrs . . . ?"

"Miss," she corrected me. "Miss Maud Williams."

Miss? An unmarried lady with a baby! Jessy and I looked through the window so the lady wouldn't see us turning red. The train stopped. The conductor must have been chasing another cow off the railroad tracks.

"Maud Williams, R.N.," said the lady. She stood up and stared down the length of the car. Only some Nahcotta ladies and an old man who lived in Ocean Park out on the beach were on board.

"What's a R.N.?" I asked.

"Registered Nurse." She sat down again, sighed, and dumped her baby onto the seat next to her so hard the bundle bounced. Horace would have howled for an hour if anybody'd put him down like that, but this baby didn't let out a peep. Miss Williams smiled at Jessy and me. "To answer your questions, girls, I've come to Nahcotta to work. I have no relations at all—anywhere in the world."

She took off her hat and put it on the seat, laughing. "Well, I guess I can relax now. It doesn't seem to me there are any mashers on this train."

And now she did the most dreadful thing I'd ever seen. She took the eight-inch-long hatpin that had anchored her hat to her hair and jabbed it right into the baby. The baby didn't yell once, though Jessy and I did—plenty.

"You *killed* it!" I cried. "The baby's dead!"

Miss Williams looked down at the blue blanket with the hatpin still quivering in it and did something more cruel and heartless. She laughed. Then she hauled out the pin, which Pa always said was "woman's most wicked weapon," and stuck it into her hat again. She picked up the baby, held it for a second, yelled "Catch!" and threw it at me.

I caught it.

The bundle was awfully light and much too soft for a baby. Horace was as solid as a brick. I was scared, but I pushed the blanket away to see the baby's face. I gasped. It was a doll! A big china-head doll in a lace-trimmed hat!

Jessy asked my question for me. "Why'd you carry a doll all the way from Missouri?"

"To discourage mashers. Mashers won't bother a woman traveling alone if she's carrying an infant in arms. Do you girls know what mashers are or are you too young?" Miss Williams looked quite fierce.

"Oh, we aren't too young! Kissin' John's a masher," said Jessy.

"Who's he?"

"The preacher's son. He's only a seventh-grader while we're eighth-graders, but he mashes plenty," I told her.

Miss Williams nodded. "Preacher's son. I might have known it." She took a crumpled letter out of her purse and asked, frowning, "Do you know a Dr. Alfred Leon Perkins?"

"Dr. Alf? Sure. He isn't a masher. We don't think he even likes ladies. He's an old bachelor."

"Well, that's good news." Miss Williams settled back on the seat. "I guess I'll be able to work with him then. He wrote the hospital where I trained that he needed a nurse, so I came West."

I was surprised. Dr. Alf hadn't told me he was getting a nurse. I wondered if she'd make calls with him.

"What'll I do with the doll?" I asked Miss Williams. "I'm over thirteen years old. I haven't got any sisters, only brothers."

"Oh, I don't know. Ebenezer's served her purpose. Give it to some little girl you know."

"I'd like it," said Jessy. "I've got a little sister."

I gave the doll to Jessy. "It could be a Christmas present. It's brand new." I doubted if Jessy's little sister would notice the doll had a pinhole in its bosom.

Jessy held the doll all the way to Nahcotta and was still carrying it when we showed Miss Williams where Dr. Alf's office was, next to the Palace Hotel. Rosinante and the buggy were outside at the hitching post, so we knew the doctor was in.

"Do you think we ought to introduce her to Dr. Alf?" Jessy asked me.

"Oh, she can take care of herself, and so can he." Then I asked, "Do you suppose that doll's got on real baby clothes, or will you have to sew them for Christmas?"

"Golly, I hope not, Amanda." She'd finished the broiler-rack newspaper holder, but was still stitching felt spectacle cases for her parents.

We went in Jessy's house through the kitchen door. Nobody was there, so we laid the doll down on the table, and Jessy took it out of the blue blanket and held it up. She went speechless! I put my hands over my mouth so I wouldn't cry out. The doll wasn't wearing baby clothes at all. It had on a dress that came to its bare toes, made of red cloth, the reddest red I'd ever seen, darker than the chest protector or the flotsam cloth!

Well, in a second Jessy and I had that doll down to its cloth body, the kitchen pump working, and the dress in a pan of water to see if it would bleed. While Jessy wrapped up the doll and ran upstairs to hide it under her bed until Christmas, I sloshed the dress up and down and round and round in the water.

"Pull it out now," Jessy ordered, breathing down my neck.

I held the dress high over the pan and I didn't see one bit of pink water dripping. When Jessy emptied the pan into the sink, the water was clear.

"Glory, hallelujah," Jessy whispered, "the Lord is still providing." She hugged me. "Oh, Amanda, that's three out of the seven reds. And they haven't cost us anything at all!"

Not much they hadn't! Almost galloping pneumonia, a perfectly good harmonica, four potatoes, and the fright of my life on the train that morning. Jessy had either stronger nerves than I did or a shorter memory.

ON DECEMBER 21 all of us went to a square dance in Nahcotta, even Horace. There I saw Maud Williams again.

She looked pretty in pale green muslin with a white lace bertha, dancing with Dr. Alf, who was a good waltzer.

She took Allan's eye right off. He asked me about her while I was standing with Jessy. "She's a R.N. from Missouri. She hates mashers." He kept trying to catch her eye, so she'd come over and ask him to dance. But she only smiled at Jessy and me, ignoring him.

Finally my brother headed straight for the nurse and asked her for the next dance, which turned out to be a polka. Polkas were so strenuous that Mama and Pa didn't even try to dance them anymore. As for Grandma, she sat with the other old ladies of her sewing circle in a row of chairs against the wall, talking about the dancers and the "poor little wallflowers nobody ever asked to dance." Pa called them "puncture" ladies, because that's what they tried to do to folks' reputations.

Allan came back after three polkas with Maud Williams. He looked winded. "She is a forceful female," he told me. "Having fun fits her like a shirt fits on a fence post."

I guessed she'd turned him down on an offer of buggy riding. Well, being snubbed might be good for him. Grandma Barnett got all the blue ribbons. Allan got all the girls. Losing once in a while might develop character in both of them.

While I was thinking of developing character, I saw John Pratt come skidding across the hall toward us Barnetts. Rats! If he asked me to dance in front of Mama, she'd make me accept to be polite. I grabbed Allan before any other Peninsula girl got to him—like Molly or Pheemie—and dragged him out onto the floor. My brother danced with me and saved me from Kissin' John, but his heart wasn't in it. He kept looking over my head and circling closer to Maud Williams as she went whirling by in a waltz with a young surfman from the Life Saving Station. She sure was cutting a swath through the Peninsula men, even if she wasn't man hankering.

I talked with her while Dr. Alf lit the tiny yellow candles on the tree and gave the little kids his Christmas lecture about not going near it and setting themselves on fire.

"You smiled at me so I guess you remember me, huh, Miss Williams?"

"I surely do. You're one of the girls I gave my baby to."

"Uh-huh, thank you. That was my big brother you just polkaed with." I pointed at Allan, who was drinking a cup of punch with Dr. Alf.

She looked as if she'd bit into a lemon. "Oh, him!"

"He isn't a masher, is he, or morally bilious?" I asked her.

"No, he's only worthless. After he told me he'd lived here all his life and doesn't hold down a job, I told him he was an overgrown youth of weak intellect."

I thought that was pretty strong, so I defended Allan. "He cleans out the barn once a week."

"Humph!" She gave my brother a queer, cross-eyed look and turned her head to talk to Molly's big, handsome Life Saving Service father. Allan had made an impression on her all right.

I left and went over to Pheemie.

"What're you grinning about?" she asked.

"Oh, nothing."

Pheemie and I stood together during the carol singing. While we sang "Hark, the Herald Angels Sing," I thought how pretty the lighted tree was and how the golden shine of the candles made the hall and the peoples' faces look golden too. I wished Mrs. Hankinson had been able to come. Jessy had asked her and said her pa would call for her in a buggy, but she'd said "no." She still coughed a little and her arthritis wasn't getting any better, so she decided not to come. We guessed that she didn't have a party dress or fancy shawl. Sometimes I thought all she had in the world were the four of us and the red rose quilt.

Mrs. Hankinson had been tickled pink when we brought her the doll dress. "Now that's what I call the right red for the second bud," she'd said, clapping her hands together. "I can't think of anything I'd rather have for a Christmas present, girls, than this."

We were pleased too, since she'd asked us not to exchange Christmas gifts with her.

But without telling me, Allan took her a gift! He had won two turkeys at the Ilwaco turkey shoot the day after the square dance. Giving her a turkey was nice of him; the next time I saw Nurse Williams I'd tell her Allan had noble impulses, even if he was lazy.

Grandma was furious about the turkey present. She gave us the rough edge of her tongue for being so considerate of Mrs. Hankinson. "It certainly appears to me that old woman down there has made all kinds of conquests in this family, hasn't she? Turning my own flesh and blood against me!" Then she thudded on her cane back to her bedroom to work on her WCTU quilt. She was coming along on it a lot faster than Mrs. Hankinson was on hers. Mrs. Hankinson was using up the cloth she had right now—the three reds and all the greens—but she was slower with her fingers than Grandma.

AUNT BEULAH LAMBERT, Pa's sister, and Uncle Paul, her husband, who lived in Portland, remembered all of us at Christmas too. Pa took the rig to Nahcotta and picked up their big package. Getting it was always the most exciting part of Christmas, because they never sent homemade presents like ours usually were. Uncle Paul was sort of rich, so Aunt Beulah shopped at Meier & Frank or Lipman Wolfe, Portland stores I'd never been in.

After I'd been "nice" about the six guest towels Grandma had made for my hope chest, and everybody had said "I think it's just beautiful" about the presents I'd made for them, we attacked Aunt Beulah's packages, all wrapped up in holly-printed paper. The presents were wonderful. Mama got a gold metal bracelet shaped like a snake crawling up her arm. Pa got an elk's tooth watch charm on a chain. Allan got a set of ivory backed hairbrushes, and Horace a silver teething ring. For me there was a butterfly muff of black velvet and white rabbit fur. Grandma's present was soft and the biggest parcel of all. I handed it to her out of the box and read aloud the note tied to it: "This is the very latest thing in Portland, Mother. It's all the rage. Love, Beulah."

We watched Grandma open her package. What could be "all the rage" in Portland? It had to be special. Aunt Beulah was very up to date—"new fangled," Pa sometimes called her. We didn't even know what some Christmas gifts she'd sent us before were and never did find out.

Grandma Barnett unwrapped her package, held up her present for less than a second, then dumped it back into the paper so nobody could see it. I got a good look, though, because I was close to her.

It was a union suit, a short-legged one, with lace at the neckline—bright red lace! The whole union suit was as red as Grandma's face was as she exploded, "That Beulah! She's taken total leave of her senses. That is the most scandalous, dreadful nether garment I have ever seen!"

"Is it made out of flannel?" I asked.

Grandma touched the hidden garment. "No, it's cotton. I think it must be a summer unmentionable. And, believe me, this is the very last time it will be mentioned in this house." She wrapped up the union suit and handed it to me. "Amanda, you dispose of this thing for me while I go write Beulah a letter telling her what I think of her citified ways. These Portland people!"

After Grandma had gone Pa said, "She means for you to take that to the kitchen and stuff it in the stove, Amanda."

"Yes, Pa."

I took it to the kitchen all right and stuffed the holly wrapping paper under a stove lid to burn. I laid the "unmentionable" out on the table and had a good look at it. No, it wasn't Turkey red cotton. The red was different— brighter. And it was good-sized. Grandma was big. So was the union suit—big in front and big in back.

In the parlor Mama had started up the music box on "Silent Night," so nobody heard me working the kitchen pump. I held a leg of the union suit under the water, counting to sixty, then squeezed the leg into a white cup. The cloth didn't bleed one bit.

While "Silent Night" tinkled to an end, I looked for a hiding place for the union suit until tomorrow and found a good one under the gunnysack Edward T. Bone slept on under the stove. I lifted him up, slid the suit under his sack, then put him back. "Sleep tight. Don't let the bedbugs bite!" I said, and patted him. Then I went back to the parlor in time for "It Came Upon a Midnight Clear" and put my hands into Aunt Beulah's lovely muff so nobody could see they were trembling because I'd disobeyed.

When the carol ended, Pa laughed and asked me, "Amanda, did you do the awful deed?"

I told him a half truth. "Yes, Pa. It got disposed of just fine."

MRS. HANKINSON was thrilled with the union suit. She didn't think it was one bit scandalous. It seemed to her a good idea—something cool to wear in hot weather. I agreed with her, but we had better uses for it. Pheemie, Molly, Jessy, and I crowded around to watch Mrs. Hankinson lay out the union suit on her table and turn it this way and that, figuring how much cloth could be got out of it. The two big problems were the front buttoning and the drop seat.

Because I was hopeful and worried about the future, I asked, "Do you think you can get two roses out of it, Mrs. Hankinson?"

She thought for a minute, then nodded. "Yes, but they

won' be big ones. I think I can get my middle-size rose that's just openin' up out of this one."

We knew the quilt pattern pretty well by now. "Then are there only the two big flowers to go?" I asked.

"Two real big ones, Amanda."

I sighed. Getting two roses out of the union suit had been a big help, but the impossible was still ahead of us. The chest protector, the flotsam from the *Geoffrey Barr*, the doll dress, and the union suit had sort of come to us without our doing much, except for trying to catch deathly colds. I had the feeling, though, that we were going to have to root-hog for those last two roses. Our luck had been too good to last much longer!

I HAD A TALK with Allan out in the barn just before New Year's Day, 1894. "How's the fancy quilt coming along down at Mrs. Hankinson's?" he asked, as we sat side by side on a hay bale.

"All right, I guess. Kind of slow. Mrs. Hankinson's got arthritis in her hands and still coughs." Her coughing was worrying me more and more. I thought she was sewing slower than last month, but that could have been my imagination because I was so eager to see the quilt finished.

Allan was glum, so to cheer him up I told him, "Mrs. Hankinson says you're a fine young man."

He was chomping on a piece of hay. "I'm glad somebody does."

"Oh, everybody does. Molly and Pheemie and Jessy like you even more, now that you made that quilting frame for Mrs. Hankinson."

"Sure, everybody does except that red-headed nurse down in Nahcotta."

I guessed it was time to tell him about her and the doll on the train, so I did. "She's sort of odd, Allan."

He didn't laugh and shook his head like he admired her all the same. "That took some spunk to come all the way out here alone." He paused, then went on. "I talked to Dr. Alf about her the other day in Oysterville. He says she's a good nurse and plans to stay on. She takes care of his office when he's out making calls." Allan kicked his heels against the hay. "Amanda, I'm leaving here pretty soon."

"On a ship out of Astoria?"

"Nope. There isn't much of a future in being a sailor. Maud says most sailors are 'footloose no-goods.' "

So he'd talked to Miss Williams again! I didn't ask how their conversation had gone. I could tell from his gloomy face. I guessed Allan was smitten with her. Mama told me she thought he might be because Miss Williams was the first girl he'd ever known who didn't fall all over him, which would get his goat all right. Mama had seemed to enjoy Allan's predicament too.

"I'm going to Portland to make something of myself, and then I'll come back here rich. Aunt Beulah'll put me up until I find work there."

I wasn't so sure. "Allan, maybe Aunt Beulah isn't speaking to us since she got that Christmas letter from Grandma."

He chuckled. "That letter was an ear blisterer all right." Grandma had read it aloud to us before she sent Allan to mail it in Nahcotta. Then he added, "Still, Aunt Beulah ought to know her own mother by now. Pa says Grandma's tongue just rolls off Beulah like water off a duck's back."

I said, "Allan, I don't understand how Pa and Aunt Beulah can be so different from Grandma. Maybe I'll ask Dr. Alf about it someday. He seems to know an awful lot of things."

He nodded. "Yep, that does beat all, don't it? I asked Dr. Alf once myself where meanness in a man or horse comes from."

"What'd he say?"

"Sometimes from bad handling when they were little, but sometimes nobody knows. He said in those cases he thinks it's the same place laziness comes from." Allan didn't smile. "I think he had me in mind when he said that. Meanness and laziness both come from the old red devil!"

THE YEAR 1894 came blowing in on another ocean storm, which fit the mood Allan and Grandma were in. Allan was moping; Grandma was yelling. She was boiling mad! Aunt Beulah had written back right away from Portland, telling Grandma that she was delighted she "liked the summer-wear union suit" and hoped she would "wear it in excellent health." I'd laughed up my sleeve over that.

After the storm was over, I took the *Oregonian* newspaper clipping Aunt Beulah had sent in her letter down to Mrs. Hankinson's.

Pheemie was already there, drinking mint tea. I asked her if she, too, wanted to hear what Mrs. Grover Cleveland wore at the New Year's reception at the White House.

"Not very much, but that won't stop you, will it?" said Pheemie.

"Not really, Euphemia." I read from the clipping: "Mrs. Cleveland was dressed in vivid magenta moiré with a bodice of Irish point lace with an artistic mass of chiffon in front. The President's wife carried no flowers."

"I don't see why she should," grumbled Pheemie. "She isn't getting married, is she?"

I ignored her. She'd rather have heard about how President Cleveland's carriage horses were harnessed. "Mrs. Hankinson, what color is magenta?"

"Red, honey, a kind of purple-red, I think."

Pheemie gave me a sideways look. "Amanda, what're you thinking about?"

"Those reds we have to get." Dramatically I quoted from a book I'd just read, borrowed from Miss Coxe. " 'I am thinking of the wild and desperate measures we may be forced to take ere long.' " Those two reds for the big roses were going to have to come out of a dry-goods store somewhere or right off somebody's back. But the dry-goods stores were out. On the back of Aunt Beulah's newspaper clipping were some Portland store ads. One of them gave the price of "first-class imported red cotton from Germany" at $1.25 a yard. Almost a king's ransom. Nobody had any money after Christmas. What's more, the tourists who paid Peninsula kids for clams and crabs weren't due until June. The quilt was due in September.

Every time I went to Mrs. Hankinson's I got more depressed. The quilting frame Allan had made her worked on pulleys and ropes. He'd fixed it real fancy. It could be lowered when she got around to doing the final quilting or raised to get it out of her way. These days the frame was up on the ceiling of the silver shack, and it hung over my head like the sword of Damocles!

ALLAN LEFT HOME the thirtieth of January, bag and baggage, for Portland. Pa and Mama and I rode down on the train to Ilwaco with him to say good-bye. We hated to see him go, but didn't try to stop him. Uncle Paul and Aunt Beulah had written that they'd be happy to put Allan up for however long it took to get him working or settled.

At the supper table the day the letter had come, Grandma snorted and said, "Then poor Beulah's going to have Allan on her hands for the rest of her days. He's no git-up-and-gitter. He's a setter in the sunshine."

Allan got up from the table and told her, "You are the most unregenerate old woman in the whole State of Washington. That's what everybody else on the Peninsula says, and I agree."

I didn't know the word "unregenerate," but at school the next day I looked it up in the dictionary. I wondered where in the world he'd learned a word that big. It was a good word for Grandma Barnett all right. The thought of her union suit going into O the Red Rose Tree kept me warm inside all the way to Ilwaco.

But I forgot about the quilt when we got off the train. The sheriff of Pacific County met us with a rifle in his hand at the train steps. Two armed deputies stood behind him. Pa stuck up his hands. "Whatever it is, Frank, no Barnett did it!" The sheriff was a great kidder, and we all knew him.

He didn't laugh, though. "Confound it, it's no joke. I'm searching all trains and boats."

"Who for?" Pa asked, getting serious.

"One a them Chinese outa the cranberry bogs. A young one by the name a Lee Bing Hung."

"What'd he do?" Allan asked.

"He mebbe killed the Boss when the Boss tried to hold back some of his pay. He hit him with a rake and skedaddled. The Boss looked to be in pretty bad shape. Dr. Alf's with him now. Nobody knows where Lee Bing Hung went to. The others in the bogs won't talk about it much."

"We met Lee Bing Hung," I told the sheriff.

"You did, huh? Where'd you see him? Has he gone north or south?"

"Oh, we met him way back in November."

"Where'd he come from before he worked up here, Amanda?"

Before I could answer "Portland," Allan spoke up. "Astoria."

"On Bond Street, then, across the Columbia? Well, that figgers. He coulda stole a rowboat at Megler and made it across the river." He turned to one of his deputies. "You go on over to Astoria and ask about him there. Get the Astoria sheriff to help you."

After the sheriff had gone aboard the train to poke around under the seats, I hauled Allan away from Pa and Mama for a second. "Allan, you told a lie to the sheriff!"

"Be quiet, Amanda. You know the Ilwaco Boss is a mean old cuss. He probably had it coming to him. He tried to hold back his pay, didn't he? I don't want Lee Bing Hung to go to jail for trying to get what was really his. I bet he was only defending himself."

"But you don't know that's how it was, Allan!" He didn't sound to me like the Allan I knew. Being sweet on Maud Williams had put sand in his craw, but maybe too much steel in his backbone. "You aren't going to get in trouble in Portland, are you, Allan?"

"What do you mean?"

"Go bad! Go to the dogs. Remember, it's a big place. Even Pa says it's full of nabobs."

Allan threw back his head and laughed. Then he pretended to have a moustache and twirled it like Simon Legree does in *Uncle Tom's Cabin*. I flung my arms around him and hugged him tight. "Be careful, Allan."

"I will, Amanda. I promise. I won't let the nabobs get me!"

# 6

# News from Portland

In FEBRUARY we started going to Mrs. Hankinson's again every Saturday afternoon because of Dr. Alf. He had met Molly and me one day in Oysterville as we were coming back from fishing in Willapa Bay. We each had a fish and a bucket of oysters we'd picked up in the sea grass at low tide. A friend of Pa's had let Molly and me go oystering in his beds.

Dr. Alf called out to us from his buggy in front of the Methodist Church. "Do you want a ride back to Nahcotta?"

"Sure," I said, though I wondered if Rosinante could pull two more people. We climbed up onto the seat next to him and put the oysters on the floor. The fish we laid across our laps, because there wasn't any room for them. Mine was a flounder which is flat, and more comfortable to hold than Molly's fish.

"Well, you're good little providers for your families, aren't you, girls? Those oysters look pretty tasty."

"Dr. Alf, we do more'n you might think," Molly told

him. "The oysters are mostly for my folks, but some of them are for Mrs. Hankinson. The fish are for her cat."

He clicked his tongue at Rosinante, who started off at a slow walk past the church and parsonage. "Yes, I've heard you girls look after Mrs. Hankinson. It's very commendable of you."

"Allan's gone now, so somebody ought to." I hesitated, then said, "We Barnetts ought to help her out."

"Why's that, Amanda?"

"Because Grandma was so mean to her. She kept her out of the church sewing circle and scared off the preacher's wife. Pheemie says she hopes Grandma gets glanders."

The doctor laughed. "It's unlikely. That's mostly a horse disease, though I have to admit your grandmother is as healthy as one."

Then he said, "I saw Mrs. Hankinson a couple of days ago. She hasn't seen you four girls much lately on Saturday afternoons."

That was true. We'd brought her food, but hadn't come to sew as we did before Christmas. "She helped us with our Christmas presents," Molly explained.

"And Christmas is over?"

I knew from his voice what he meant, so I told him, "We aren't really crazy about doing fancywork."

"Hmmm."

For a long time Rosinante went along in the ruts and nobody said anything. Then all at once Dr. Alf spoke up, "I think you girls ought to go back to Mrs. Hankinson's on Saturdays to sew. Go as long as she wants you to." He gave each of us a frown. "She needs you, even if you don't need her. She's a very remarkable woman, you know."

"Oh, we know," agreed Molly.

"And a fine seamstress, too, with a lot to teach you. And she's very old. She needs company, like so many older folks do."

The way he spoke made me feel guilty and sad. We hadn't been able to find a color-true red for over six weeks, and I was losing heart.

Dr. Alf drove Molly and me all the way to the top of the dune above the silver shack. "Thank you, Dr. Alf," I said.

"Thank you, Rosinante," Molly joked.

But the doctor didn't laugh. "Are you going Saturdays?"

I looked at Molly. "All right," we both promised. Then I asked, "Is Mrs. Hankinson awful sick?"

"No, but she's not robust either. Her cough doesn't go away, and this ocean air's bad for her." Now he smiled. "Be good to her. Sometimes a little attention's better for a person than a pail of pills. Besides, you do want to get that red rose quilt done in time for the County Fair, don't you?"

I gasped but kept my head. Molly, though, blurted out, "Jessy Reed told you! She tattled!"

"No, Mrs. Hankinson, herself, is the culprit. She showed me the quilt blocks she was doing. I thought I recognized the cloth in one of those rosebuds. It brought Jessy to mind. She took it remarkably well when I told her I'd given away the gift her mother made for me."

"Oh, other things in the quilt are lots worse than the chest protector," said Molly.

I added, now that the secret was out, "Some of them are unmentionable. Good-bye, Dr. Alf. Give our regards to Miss Williams. Please tell her we haven't heard yet from Allan, but at least he hasn't written home for money."

"I will, Amanda, and please tell your father to come by my office in the next couple of days with his team and wagon. I've got a heavy favor to ask of him." He looked again at his old waltz-playing watch, sighed, and drove off back to Nahcotta.

I sort of folded my flounder into my oyster bucket, grabbed Molly's arm, and we hauled ourselves over Mrs. Hankinson's sand dune. At the bottom of the dune I said, "That was doctor's orders he gave us. We have to learn to sew better and bring fish and find those other reds. I think we're going to be pretty busy!"

"Oh, Amanda, I'm not dumb. I know that."

MARCH WENT BY with nothing happening except that we were getting to be better sewers, according to Mrs. Hankinson. And we found out why Dr. Alf had wanted Pa to come by with the wagon—to haul a new stove down to the silver shack. Rust was a terrible problem on the Peninsula. Mrs. Hankinson's old stove was rusting apart, and because she had to cook and keep warm, Dr. Alf gave her a stove as a present.

We girls thought that was mighty kind of him. So did Pa and Mama, who kept it secret from Grandma. She would have had something nasty to say.

I told Dr. Alf one day in Nahcotta how nice I thought he was. All he said was, "Well, if you girls can get a blue ribbon for the old lady, I guess I can do something, too, can't I?"

"Dr. Alf, I'm worried that we won't be able to get the other red cloth she needs in time for the County Fair."

He frowned, then said, "Well, Amanda, I can't help you there. You've already acquired the only red I have to give. I don't know word one about cloth. I never made a quilt in my life either. The only thing I ever sewed up were people, like the boss of the cranberry pickers back in January. I did a good job on that old cuss. He's right as rain. Good day, Amanda." He tipped his hat and went into the Palace Hotel before I could tell him more of our troubles.

APRIL CAME IN NICE and mild, with no shipwrecks or sickness. And no red cotton cloth "falling down from heaven," as Molly put it. We were jumpy as fleas on a hot rock by the middle of the month when Miss Coxe announced that the Oysterville eighth grade had challenged the Nahcotta eighth grade to a spelling bee. All of us had to compete.

I put up my hand. "What's the prize if we win?"

"Money?" asked Pheemie.

"There's no prize, girls, just the honor of it all." Miss Coxe was mad. "I'm certainly surprised at you! I'll expect the two of you to study particularly hard now that I see you're so eager to win."

I sighed. I wanted money to buy cloth, if that was the only way we could get it. I didn't even laugh when Pheemie whispered to me behind Miss Coxe's back, "I'll bet there's a second prize. A big kiss from Kissin' John."

Mama coached me with words from the Montgomery Ward's catalog, the Bible, and Sir Walter Scott. I was a good natural speller, but I was mighty nervous as Molly, Jessy, Pheemie, and I piled into a wagon with the other eighth-graders for Oysterville.

The schoolhouse there had been built under a black walnut tree. Along one side of the building was a rose-bush already in bloom, and seeing the yellow roses made me feel mighty low. As I lined up against one wall with the other Nahcotta kids and looked across the room at the Oysterville eighth-graders, I became more mournful. Mama and Pa, Grandma Barnett, Dr. Alf, Miss Williams, and the Preacher Pratts were sitting in the middle of the schoolhouse at the desks, which were too small for everybody but Kissin' John, who was runty.

Jessy, next to me, whispered, "They have come to witness our downfall!"

First the Oysterville teacher introduced an old man with a gray beard. We knew who he was—half owner of the railroad and owner of whole acres of oyster beds out in Willapa Bay. The teacher called him a "captain of industry" and a "pillar of society." I figured he was a nabob for sure.

The old man ran the spelling bee. First, he'd give a word to the Oysterville side, then a word to one of us from Nahcotta. Our three boys were spelled down right off and went to sit at desks, where they made faces at the four of us girls left standing. Pretty soon there were just three girls and one boy left on the Oysterville side.

Molly got spelled down on "excellent," and an

Oysterville girl on "treachery." Then Pheemie sat down after missing "edible," which made Jessy giggle. The next Oysterville girl was spelled out on "doggerel." That left only two on each side: Jessy and me, and a tall, skinny girl and a fat boy with big, bulging eyes and a pursed-up mouth. Now the words got longer and harder. The Oysterville girl lost on "sociability," which I spelled right off. Then the old "captain of industry" gave Jessy "separative." That cooked her goose, and down she went, leaving me and the boy staring at each other and everybody in the schoolhouse holding his breath.

The tough words came at me thick and fast, making me shake and sweat. Even Grandma Barnett was yelling "Hurray for Nahcotta" and stamping her cane on the floor when I got another word right. Finally the old man turned to the back of his book where the horrible words were. He read off "unmentionable" to the Oysterville boy. That ended him. He put in a "u" in place of the "a." I spelled it right off, keeping my eyes on the ceiling, because I could hear my three friends giggling.

I'd won! While everybody clapped, I blushed and was about to sit down next to Molly when the old "pillar of society" held up his hand for quiet. "I think for the honor of the male sex and Oysterville, I'll spell this little lady down myself." He handed the book to Dr. Alf, who sat in the front row, and walked over to the Oysterville side of the schoolhouse, facing me.

Everybody applauded like mad, except my friends who thought this wasn't fair. From the look on his face, neither did Dr. Alf, but he went along with the idea. "Are you ready, Amanda?" he asked me. "Are you ready, sir?" he asked the old man.

The "captain of industry" was a dandy speller all right. We went through a dozen words like "exhibition," "pecuniary," and "dessert," and then Dr. Alf closed the book. He looked at the old man. "Sir, please spell 'sesquicentennial.'"

He started out just fine, then got all confused. He hesitated.

"Come on now," said the doctor.

"S-e-s-q-u-i-c-e-n-t-e-n-i-a-l," spelled the old man.

"Wrong!" shouted Dr. Alf.

Every head turned to me. I closed my eyes, prayed, and spelled it the way I saw it in my head, even if I didn't know what the word meant.

There was silence for a moment, then Dr. Alf shouted, "Correct! Nahcotta is the winner! Amanda Ann Barnett wins!"

Everybody went wild. They cheered and cheered while I got red some more. While we had punch and cookies, people congratulated me. The old man came up, too, and shook my hand. "You're a pretty good speller, little lady. You deserve a reward." Then he moved right off to talk to some oystermen about next year's reseeding.

Maud Williams, who'd heard what he said, told me, "You do deserve a reward. That was good work."

"Thank you."

"I think the old man should have given you something, don't you?" asked the nurse.

"I guess so."

"Well, he won't—the old capitalist." She sipped her punch. "His kind never does, the old grabbers." She winked at me. "How do you think the rich get rich? By never giving anything away, that's how."

I didn't think she was exactly fair. "Oh, they aren't all like that, Miss Williams. My uncle up in Portland's a rich man. My brother's living with him and our aunt now."

"Oh, is Allan gone? I hadn't noticed." Miss Williams drifted off to talk with Miss Coxe.

Rats! It'd been a horrible day even if I had won for Nahcotta.

While we made May baskets the next day, the four of us put an evil spell on the old "captain of industry"—not that our spells ever had worked.

As Pheemie and I gathered sweet-smelling white strawberry blossoms to fill the woven paper baskets, she told me, "He should have given you some money for all that good spelling you did, Amanda. If he had, we could have bought the reds we need. I hope he gets black leg. That's a sheep disease."

When we told Mrs. Hankinson about the spelling bee, she was tickled that I'd won. "Good for you, Amanda. Lots a folks can't even read, let alone spell. Be thankful you can do both of 'em."

"Yes, ma'am," I said, while she sniffed the flowers we'd brought her in the May baskets.

We didn't mention that we hadn't come up with one red for O the Red Rose Tree since the day before Christmas, and she hadn't asked us. She was still coughing, and it seemed to me that sometimes her hands trembled when she sewed.

THE WEATHER IN MAY was real nice, and I wished I could be out Saturdays picking up moonstones and agates on the beach or digging clams rather than sewing down in the silver shack. I was getting pretty discouraged. So was Jessy. She said to me one afternoon as I walked home from school with her, "Amanda, I have given up all hope of success, I think."

"Me, too."

She sighed. We were at her folks' store by now. "Well, Amanda, come in. Pa'll give us some horehound candy or butterballs, if I ask him."

I didn't need to be invited anywhere twice for candy. Mr. Reed was too busy to say no when Jessy asked him about the candy. He was talking with a man, a derby-hatted gentleman in a black-and-white checkered suit, handlebar moustache, long sideburns, and a strong smell of bay rum from a barber shop.

"He's a drummer from Portland," Jessy told me.

I paid no attention to him until I heard him say, "Well, Mr. Reed, how you fixed for cloth? I got samples today of some of the finest cotton made in Europe."

I stopped with my hand halfway down the butterball jar. Cotton cloth from Europe?

"Nope, I don't need cloth this time around," Mr. Reed told him.

Then Jessy cried out, "Pa, Mama wants a new dress for her birthday—not a catalog one this time, remember!"

"Drat, I almost forgot. You're right, Jessamine. Since your Ma's gone visiting in Ilwaco, I guess now's the time to get the cloth as a surprise for her." Mr. Reed was real nice. He waved for us to come over. "Well, you girls know more about such matters than I do. You know your Ma's taste, Jessy. You pick out the yard goods for her."

Jessy and I ran behind the counter. "We'll see that cloth from Europe," she told the drummer, "but we won't look at calico or anything else. No printed cloth at all, mind you."

He chuckled. "Here's a little lady who knows her mind!"

"I sure do," said Jessy.

He took a little book of cloth samples out of his straw suitcase and put it on the counter, but before he could open it, Mr. Reed said, wrinkling his forehead, "I think, Jessy, your ma wanted serpent-green or gray."

"Dove-gray, Pa, was what Mama said."

"I got 'em both." The drummer opened the sample book to show us a sick-looking yellowish green. I shuddered. That was serpent-green sure enough.

"Now which color's that, green or gray?" asked Mr. Reed.

I opened my mouth to gasp, but Jessy pinched me, hissing, "Shut up. Let me do the talking, Amanda."

The drummer didn't seem surprised at Mr. Reed's not knowing the difference. He said, "This here's serpent. It's number eight, very stylish up in Portland."

"Mama wouldn't like it, Pa," said Jessy. She grabbed the book, thumbed through it to the reds, and stopped at one so bright blue-red it made me want to sneeze. "This is what Mama'd like."

"But that's bright—" the salesman started to protest.

"This is what Mama really wants," Jessy interrupted. "Six yards of it."

Mr. Reed pulled the book over to himself. He stroked the red cloth, then nodded. "It's good quality. This is what she'd like, you say, Jessy?"

"That's it, Pa."

"Well, then," he told the drummer, "write up the order."

The salesman gave Jessy a queer look, shrugged his shoulders, and took out an order pad and pencil. He wrote down six yards of number twenty-three.

"You think that'll make up into a nice dress?" Mr. Reed asked the drummer.

"That will make a fine . . . uh . . . real nice dress. Nobody who sees your wife wearing it will ever forget it. But then different folks see things in different ways. The cloth'll be here in ten days." The man gave Jessy another odd look, packed up his stuff, and left.

I kept quiet, my mouth full of butterball, while Jessy and her pa talked. "Do you think your mother'll like that?" He was grinning. "It was a nice shade of gray, wasn't it?"

"It sure was, Papa—dove-gray."

I choked on my butterball. Gray? He thought red was gray?

While Jessy pounded me on the back to get the butterball down, she whispered, "Keep quiet. Pa's red-and-green color-blind. Reds are all gray to him. He's made lots of mistakes on things because of it. Mama tells him what waistcoat to wear every morning."

"But your ma'll kill you when she finds out, Jessy! No lady on the Peninsula would wear a red dress like that!"

Jessy rolled her eyes toward heaven. "She'll only half kill me if I'm lucky. I'll tell her I think my eyes are going bad on me because I'm aging and I'm getting sort of color-blind, too. I'll tell her I think it runs in the family."

"Oh, Jessy!"

"You be quiet, Amanda. Maybe Mama'll send the cloth back, but before she does I'll cut off half a yard of it. She can take it out of my hide making me scrub floors if she wants to. No matter! We've got the sixth rose for Mrs. Hankinson, haven't we?"

"I guess so, but it was just awful the way you did it, Jessy."

She whirled on me, "Now you listen to me, Amanda Barnett! Pa's real touchy about being color-blind. There's a good chance Mama won't dare send the red cloth back at all and will use it for something else, like maybe more chest protectors or kitchen curtains. She'll think it was his mistake and never say a word about it." She stamped her foot. "You have to admit, by hook or by crook, I did it!"

"By *crook* you did it, Jessamine Reed!"

JESSY GOT SWITCHED by her mother when the red cloth arrived, but Mr. Reed never learned it wasn't dove-gray. Mrs. Reed put it away, telling him she'd take it to the Oysterville seamstress pretty soon, meaning never, and that was the end of that. Except that Jessy cut off a piece for

O the Red Rose Tree, figuring it'd never be missed, and hid it under her bed. The next Saturday she smuggled the cloth out folded on top of her head under her sunbonnet.

Mrs. Hankinson threw up her hands when she saw the piece of cloth. "Land a mercy, Jessamine, I think that's one of the purtiest reds I ever did see."

"It's imported from Europe," said Jessy, with cream on her whiskers again, "and it won't bleed one bit."

"Only one more rose to go!" put in Molly.

"Oh, we'll get that one too," promised Jessy. Power had gone to her head.

I kept quiet. It'd been a long dry spell from December to May. We couldn't let that long a time go by again for the last red. The Fair was going to be held on the third of September.

Mrs. Hankinson put the red cloth away and went to make us mint tea while we worked on samplers she'd thought up for us. We had written her sayings in ink on cloth and were sewing them for "practice." Jessy's was "Honesty Is the Best Policy." Her motto made me want to laugh.

While I was winding up a French knot on my embroidery needle, Mrs. Hankinson suddenly asked me, "How's that handsome brother a yours, Amanda?"

Allan hadn't written a line to us, and Mama was fit to be tied. Pa was fuming, while Grandma was laughing up her sleeve. She'd said he'd never pick up a pen once he hit Portland. I missed him. So did poor old Edward T. Bone, who went up to Allan's room every morning, looking for him, wagging his tail with hope. I said, "Aunt Beulah wrote us that he showed up and stayed with her and Uncle Paul for a while. Then he rented a houseboat on the Willamette River and got a job. And that was the last she saw of him." I sighed. "Grandma says he's gone to the dogs!"

"Nonsense!" snapped Mrs. Hankinson. Oh, she was mad—the first time I'd seen her angry. Her eyes popped off blue sparks. "Don' you pay no need to what she says. There's good stuff in that boy."

"Won't he ever come back, Amanda?" asked Pheemie.

"I don't know, Euphemia. Maybe the dogs have got him, but he can't ever say I didn't warn him!"

When I got home that day, Mama was sitting on the front porch holding Horace on her lap. She beckoned to me to hurry so I ran. "Beulah wrote us again," she called out before I reached the porch.

"What'd she say about Allan?" I knew by Mama's smile that the news was good.

"He called on Beulah and Paul last week. He's just fine, working in a bank in Portland."

That fit. Allan was a good arithmeticker. "Is he still living on the river?"

"Yes, but it's a nice houseboat. Beulah was there last week to chaperone when Allan took Lorelei to visit it."

"Lorelei? Who's she?"

"The girl Allan's courting." Mama was laughing at Horace, who was leaning over, trying to grab sleeping Edward T. Bone's bushy tail. "She's Lorelei Withington, a banker's daughter."

Well, that made sense too. If the banker Allan worked for had a daughter and she spied Allan, she'd be after him hammer and tongs. But I doubted if she'd grab him. Allan would be plenty wary of nabobs after my warning. Bankers were great big nabobs! "I'm sure glad he's all right," I told· Mama, "but I wish he'd write us himself."

Mama wasn't listening to me as she went after Horace, who had rolled off her lap onto the porch. He had Edward T. Bone's tail in both hands and was lifting it up to bite it. Mama grabbed Horace while I hauled the dog by his front quarters off the porch. Horace yelled so loud that I didn't get to talk to Mama about Allan anymore.

NOTHING NEW happened for a couple of days. Then one Saturday morning Pa came back from Nahcotta and the post office. I thought he looked queer as he got down out of the buggy.

"What's wrong, Pa? You sick?"

"It's Allan." He struck his breast, scaring me, but then I saw he was beating on his pocket, not his heart. Sticking out of the top of his pocket was an envelope. All I could think of that would make Pa look so strained was that Allan had robbed the bank he was working for.

He said, "Allan's getting married."

"To the banker's daughter?"

"Yep, she's the one." He shook his head. "I never thought Allan would up and do the deed. He popped the question and she accepted. Now he'll probably stay in Portland forever."

"I bet she popped it, and he didn't dare say no."

"I don't know, Amanda. I'd had hopes Allan would get

his fill of Portland after a while and come back to the Peninsula."

"But, Pa, you wanted him to go to Portland!"

He gave me a sharp look. "You women are changing your minds all the time. It's supposed to be a female privilege. Can't a man do it, too?" He unhitched our sorrel mare and slapped her rump so she'd trot into her stall in the barn. "Come on, Amanda, we'll break the news to your ma and grandma."

Grandma read Allan's letter out loud, which didn't take long:

Dear Folks,
   I'm fine. How are you?
     Love,
      Allan
P.S. I'm marrying a girl by the name of Lorelei Withington early next month here in Portland. Come up if you want to see me take the fatal plunge.

Mama didn't say anything, but looked mournfully at Pa. I knew she'd missed Allan and wanted him home too. Grandma, though, was beside herself with happiness.

"By the great lord Harry, he went and did it! I never dreamed he'd have the gumption. A banker's daughter! Now there's a real catch for any man. Allan'll make his fortune yet." She looked at Pa. "I'm thinking of attending the nuptials. How about you, Charles?"

Pa worried his moustache, then told her, "Can't, Ma.

The milkers won't let me. Cows don't give a hoot about nuptials."

"Well, then, the Barnett ladies will represent the family," Grandma declared.

"Me too?" I asked.

"You, too, Amanda, and Horace. It isn't each and every day a Barnett lands a banker's daughter." Grandma got up from her rocker and started upstairs. On the landing she turned around and called down, "I'm going to pack now. We'll leave right away and stay with Beulah. I can spare the time. My WCTU quilt's all done for the County Fair. I can stay all summer!"

*Quilt!* All at once the bottom dropped out of my stomach. Portland—all summer! I'd be deserting the cause before we had the last red. Mrs. Hankinson wasn't anywhere near done. This was awful—just awful!

# 7

## *Out Among the Nabobs*

I WENT DOWN to the silver shack just as soon as I could. I wanted to be there first that Saturday afternoon and tell Mrs. Hankinson I was going away. I was torn twixt and tween, wanting to see Allan and wanting to stay home and try to get the last red.

She heard what I had to say, then told me, "Amanda, it seems to me you better go. You don' lose a brother ev'ry day."

"Lose one?"

She nodded. "There's a old sayin', 'A daughter's a daughter all of her life; a son's a son till he takes a wife.' That's true. When they do, they don' write home no more. They get devil-may-care of their homefolks. That's how it was with my youngest. Wasn' till his wife died I ever knew where he'd gone to. And then he sent for me to keep house for him."

"Oh," I guessed she'd had a sad life. "But you were real happy with Lovin' George, weren't you?"

"Lovin' George? What?" She stared at me, then started to chuckle. "Oh, you mean my husband, don' you? No, dear, Lovin' George's only some man in a old-time song he used to sing. My husband was named Joseph. Yes, honey, I was happy with him when my boys were young'uns."

"But it didn't last, huh?"

"For a while it did." She was rocking and looking up at Allan's quilt frame on her ceiling. "Happiness is a some-time thing, Amanda. When it comes along, you grab hold and hang on tight long as you can. It gen'rally don' last too long. Mis'ry, on the other hand, can come to stay, and there ain't a broom in the world that can sweep it out sometimes."

"I sure hope you aren't too miserable now," I told her.

She reached out and patted my arm. "Not no more, Amanda. That's because of you and the other girls. And you know, that red rose quilt put heart back into me."

"But with me gone maybe we can't get the red for the last rose!"

She was quiet for a while, then said, "It ain't the place a person's goin' to that's most important; it's the journeyin' to it." She smiled at me. "I don' expect you understand that, do you? Not yet anyhow. You got to live some more. Some folks never find it out, but I don' think you're gonna be one a them. Don' you fret about the rose tree quilt. If there's to be a seventh red rose, there will be. After all, you're movin' to new huntin' grounds, ain't you?"

It was as though somebody lit a light in my head. I would have told Mrs. Hankinson what I was thinking, but just then Jessie and Pheemie came knocking. I waited until

Molly was there, too, then told them about Allan and our going to Portland to his wedding.

"Golly, Amanda, what about the quilt?" Molly asked, when Mrs. Hankinson went outside to call Jocelyn in for the piece of fish Pheemie'd brought him.

"Well, what about it, Molly? You can root-hog for the red cloth down here while I root-hog up in Portland."

"There ought to be yards and yards of it at Meier & Frank," said Jessy, who'd been to Portland.

"Sure, Jessamine, and I know what it costs too. Remember I've seen *Oregonian* ads."

"Maybe your Aunt Beulah'll give you the money to buy cloth if she's as rich as you say she is," put in Pheemie.

"Maybe she might, but Aunt Beulah's a gabber." I'd got to know her when she visited us two years ago. "She might let it out to Grandma why I wanted the cloth, and then I'd really be in a mess, and wouldn't get the cloth either." An even more horrible thought came to me.

"Imagine what Aunt Beulah might think about the red union suit she sent Grandma showing up in scraps in O the Red Rose Tree. She might get wildly mad. No, I will have to get that red by secret hook or by crook."

"I sure hope it'll be by crook," said Jessy, as she took up "Honesty Is the Best Policy" and started to embroider.

I looked at my sampler, which read, "Where There's a Will, There's a Way." That would be my Portland motto!

BOARDING THE TRAIN on May 30, we Barnett females and Horace ran into Dr. Alf and Nurse Williams in Nahcotta. They were headed for the Doctor's buggy, but stopped when they saw us and our suitcases.

"Well, well, it looks like a mass exodus of Barnetts," said Dr. Alf. "What're you doing, deserting husband and father?"

Grandma spoke for all of us. "No, Alfred, We're off to Portland. Allan is getting married." She bobbed her head at Miss Williams, grinning. "He's made a real smart catch, a banker's daughter. That's what I call good connections!" Grandma knew about Miss Williams and Allan.

I didn't want to look at the nurse's face, but I did. She didn't bat an eyelash at Grandma's mean bragging. "That's nice," she said and left, going to the buggy.

Dr. Alf stayed behind. "I take it Allan won't be coming back home then?"

"Oh, no, he has an excellent position in a bank in Portland," Grandma explained.

"Well, then, convey my felicitations to the newlyweds." Dr. Alf started off. I dropped my suitcase and ran after him. "Take good care of Mrs. Hankinson, please, while I'm gone."

"I try to take good care of all of my patients, Amanda."

I would have told him about our trouble with the last red, but just then the train whistle hooted. Grandma screeched over it, "Amanda, you get on board this very minute or we'll miss the boat!"

At the Astoria wharf we took the *T.J. Potter*, the side-wheeler steamer that made the Portland run. The boat was nice, lots nicer than the one we always went on to cross the Columbia. There were cabins we could sleep in overnight. I got stuck in one with Grandma, so of course I stayed up on deck as long as I could, running from the Washington side to the Oregon side to see what I could see.

Finally one of the deckhands told me, "Quit rockin' the boat, little lady." I certainly wasn't heavy enough to do that, so I sniffed and turned away, hoping he'd leave. He didn't. He stayed and gave me a talking-to about how dangerous and swift the Columbia River was in case anybody fell in. I already knew that and told him so.

He pointed to a white-painted farmhouse on the Oregon side. "You see that place?"

"Sure."

"That house oughta be a hundred yards farther back from the river, even if it is low tide right now. The Columbia's risin'."

"Doesn't it always rise in the spring?" Miss Coxe had told us the Columbia rose in Canadian mountains and that melting snow made the water level of the river go up in the spring.

"Sure it does," the man told me, "but not this fast. I never saw anythin' like it. Neither did the cap'n in all his years on the river."

I looked over the side of the *T.J. Potter.* A lot of flotsam—pieces of wood and what looked to me like a whole chicken coop—was going by on its way to the Pacific Ocean. Because I knew we were fighting the current going up to Portland, I asked him, "Won't we get to Portland?"

"We'll git there, but mebbe we're gonna be in for a flood, a big one this time."

A flood! Oh, my! I went below to tell Grandma and

Mama. Mama seemed worried, but Grandma only *humphed* and went on crocheting. "In my time," she said, "I've seen a fire in Missouri, a tornado in Kansas, blight in Texas, and gales in Washington State, but never a flood. The river didn't look particularly high to me at Astoria. You're just chattering again, girl. I'll believe a flood when we see it. Besides, Portland is on the Willamette River, not the Columbia."

I didn't remind her that the Willamette was connected to the Columbia, and the Columbia's water could back up, so maybe there could be a flood. I wondered about it all night in my bunk while she snored in hers. Would a flood strand us in Portland for weeks and weeks? Finally I fell asleep around dawn, about the time the *T.J. Potter* passed Saint Helens, skirted the east edge of Sauvies Island, and steamed from there into one of the mouths of the Willamette. At eleven o'clock in the morning we came to Portland.

And oh, the Willamette was flooded! It was so hot on the deck of the *T.J. Potter* that I was perspiring. I was scared, too, and excited. We went under two bridges, sailing at slow speed, with the captain sounding his ship's bells as the drawbridges opened. I looked up as we passed under. Men were standing on the steel Morrison Street bridge with long poles, ready to push off flotsam that might get tangled in the drawbridge section and jam it.

Once we cleared both bridges, a little sidewheeler came up to hail the *T.J. Potter*. Her captain had a ship's horn. "Ahoy, the *T.J. Potter!*" he shouted. "Try not to make any more waves than you need to. Front Street's flooded. You'll have to disembark your passengers in rowboats at the wharf."

"When's high water expected?" our captain called down.

"In twenty-four hours if we're lucky." Then the side-wheeler steamed off to warn more boats coming into Portland.

At last I could see Portland. The city was on both sides of the muddy Willamette, with mostly little wooden houses on the left side and fancy, tall brick-and-stone business buildings, some with towers, on the right. In the background on the right was a big green ridge, and below it were houses all the way down to the Willamette's edge.

Soon we came to the *T.J. Potter*'s wharf, but all I could see was a bunch of hogsheads and barrels sitting in a couple of feet of water. Our captain must have had a pretty good idea where the dock and pilings were, or else he gauged the location by the men standing around the barrels in hip boots. He brought the steamer in just fine, then blew the ship's whistle, while the deckhands went below to get our baggage.

The whistles brought eight rowboats down to the dock.

"Now how in the world will we get into those?" asked Grandma, irritated.

I giggled. "We can't use a gangplank. I guess we'll have to go down the ship's ladder the way those sailors are doing."

Mama went down the ladder into a skiff first, and then a sailor brought Horace to her. He came back and helped Grandma, who was scared she'd fall. I climbed down last.

Our boatman caught Grandma's cane in midair when a deckhand threw it to him. Then he told us, "This'll cost you folks a dollar. I'll let you off on Second Street. First Street's flooded now too."

"A dollar!" Grandma exploded. "You're a bandit!"

A helmeted policeman in hip boots standing near us said, "That's the going rate today, ma'am."

The rower grinned, swung the skiff away from the barrels, and rowed off the wharf.

I looked around at Portland. The brick buildings on Front and First Streets had striped awnings up just like Astoria stores had in hot weather. Everybody who was walking around wore hip boots, but most folks were in boats like ours. Siphon pumps were going in front of some places. Men were hammering up homemade signs, *Business as Usual, Second Floor, Please, Enter Through the Window.* Other men were laying down plank walkways over the flooded streets, so people wouldn't have to wear boots. From the way the Columbia and Willamette had looked to me, the walkways would be floating soon.

At Second Street, Mama paid the boatman while Horace struggled to get out of her arms and run off to wade in the water. Meanwhile, Grandma hired a hansom cab waiting at the flood's edge.

"We're going to Nineteenth Street," she told the driver, and gave him Aunt Beulah's address. When we were jammed inside, she asked him, "How long has this dreadful flood been going on?"

"Not too long. The river came up lots faster'n we'd guessed it would, lady." He looked worried. "The flood's makin' lots of trouble—businesses underwater, houseboats breakin' loose from their moorings and headin' toward Oregon City."

"Allan!" Mama cried out.

I comforted her. "Oh, don't worry about him. I'll bet he knew what to do when the flood started."

"What would he do?"

"Move back in with Aunt Beulah."

"Oh, dear, I hope so."

The cab driver went on talking, "Folks are scared of fevers comin' after the water goes down. Travelers are stranded. The railroad tracks are underwater. The train station's three feet under. You should hear some a them Italians from the op'ry company celebratin' up at the Portland Hotel 'cause they're high and dry."

I wasn't interested in Italians. I was thinking of Allan, hoping he'd had the good sense I'd told Mama he had. We went uphill all the way to Nineteenth Street and finally stopped at a white house with a circular driveway and an iron deer standing near a fountain on the front lawn. The house was sure elegant with bay windows, two balconies, and gingerbread trim. Roses were in bloom all around the front porch—lots of red ones. Seeing them made me homesick, but I guessed I'd have to harden myself to the sight of roses. After all, Portland was the Rose City.

Aunt Beulah must have been looking out the window because she came running out to us, her arms wide open. "Oh, you've come! I've been worried you wouldn't because of the flood. And you brought Baby Horace, too, and Baby Amanda!"

Aunt Beulah hadn't seen me for a couple of years, and it was plain she didn't remember me much. She was plumper and had some gray in her brown hair, but when she hugged me she still smelled nice, of orange flower water. And she was as elegant as I remembered her, this time in a Nile-green tea gown.

"Where's Allan?" was the first thing Mama asked.

"He moved back with Paul and me last night. His sweet little houseboat floated away from under the Third Avenue bridge up onto somebody's stoop on First Street, so he had to leave."

"Thank heaven!"

Aunt Beulah went on talking as she led us inside her house. If I'd thought the outside looked good, the inside looked better. There were marble-topped tables, flowered carpets, alabaster and marble statues, big gilt-framed mirrors, green velvet draperies with gold tassels. And a Chinese houseboy in black silk trousers and jacket was standing at the foot of the wide stairs. When he saw us, he bowed.

"This is Ching," Aunt Beulah told us. "You all must be absolutely exhausted. He'll show you to your rooms, so you can freshen up before lunch and get out of your corsets."

Ching bowed again. Suddenly a bell jangled somewhere in the house. Ching leaped a foot into the air. So did Aunt Beulah. Then she laughed. "I don't think Ching or I will ever get used to that. Paul insisted we get one two years ago."

"Used to what?" Grandma asked, as the bell went on jangling.

"The telephone, Mother."

Telephone! Golly. I'd read about them, but had never seen one.

"Oh, yes, Mother, there are nearly a hundred telephones in Portland. They're quite common now," said Aunt Beulah, when the thing stopped ringing. Then it started right up again. She cocked her head to one side, listening. "Well, it *is* for us. Eight rings. I guess I'd better go see who is on the other end of it." She flung up her hands and hurried down the hall.

Grandma snorted while Ching picked up our suitcases. "That's Beulah for you! Always has to have the latest thing. New-fangled. Fads. Imagine standing around counting up to eight all day long."

We followed Ching upstairs with Horace fretting. He'd gone to sleep in the hansom cab, but the telephone bell woke him up. He and Mama went into a room first, then Grandma into another, and finally Ching showed me my room.

I wasn't half as interested in it as I was in the telephone, even if it was the fanciest room I'd ever seen, with green ruffles and white muslin everywhere and a shiny, green satin bedspread. I hoped before we left Portland I'd get to talk on the telephone. Maybe Grandma was wrong, and it wouldn't be a fad. Some new-fangled things did last— electric street lights for instance. Even Astoria had those. They were useful.

Aunt Beulah came bustling in while I was unpacking. "You certainly aren't Baby Amanda anymore, are you, dear? You're grown. You're very pretty, you know. There doesn't seem to be much Barnett in you at all, thank heaven. I was always worried I'd have a daughter who'd be all big-boned Barnett!" She came closer. "Tell me, what did you think of the scarlet union suit I sent your grandmother for Christmas?"

"I liked it just fine, Aunt Beulah."

She patted my shoulder. "That's good, dear. I'm glad to see you're modern-minded." She whisked back a curtain and showed me a metal thing that looked as if it had been pleated. "That's a radiator, dear. It gives off steam heat."

"Who was on the other end of the telephone?" I couldn't help asking. I didn't want any more heat than Portland already had naturally.

"Your brother from the bank. I told him you were all safely here, but your father, and he said he'd ring up Miss Withington at home. They have only four rings, the lucky people. The Withingtons want to meet all of you tonight at their house, and I'll arrange a yellow breakfast in your honor at once."

"Tonight at the Withingtons, and a yellow breakfast?"

"Oh, yes, Amanda, the telephone speeds up things wonderfully. We use engraved invitations for only formal events."

I'd never even seen an engraved invitation. "When do I go to see Meier & Frank and Lipman Wolfe and the other stores, Aunt Beulah? Are they underwater, too?"

"Not yet, dear. We trust they won't be. After all, we must deck you out properly if you and Jerome are to be members of the wedding and on public display for the cream of society to see."

"Jerome? Who's that?"

"Lorelei's little brother. He's eight years old, I believe, but acts much, much older. Quite the little gentleman, and so musical."

Member of the wedding? Public display for the cream of society? Nabobs for sure! I'd barely got through the Oysterville spelling bee in one piece. A wedding would be worse. Pa'd told me once out in the barn that he'd never for a minute regretted marrying Mama, but he'd be danged if he'd go through a church wedding again, even for her. He said church weddings had been dreamed up by the mothers of the bride, who were the only folks who really enjoyed them and wanted guests' presents as much as their presence. He'd offered me a whole hundred dollars in gold if I'd elope when the time came for me to get married. I'd agreed I would.

AT SIX O'CLOCK Allan came in with Uncle Paul, who was a tall, thin, red-faced man. Allan hugged us all, even Grandma, who complained he'd crushed one of her short ribs. Allan was sure that Horace remembered him "perfectly well" and said I was two inches taller. He looked fine, handsome as ever, in a dark suit exactly like Uncle Paul's.

At dinner Grandma wanted to talk about Lorelei and the wedding, but the men held her down. Allan joshed her, "Now, Grandma, it isn't every day Portland has a flood. It has weddings all the time." Then he turned serious. "The flood's getting worse. They expected high water by tomorrow, but it looks now as if it'll come later than that. Third

Street'll be underwater by tomorrow. I'm going to work as usual, but I think I'll have to put the stool in my teller's cage on stilts to keep my feet dry."

"When and where are you getting married?" Grandma busted in.

"Trinity Church where the Withingtons go. That's on Sixth and Oak." Allan smiled at me. "Maybe we'll get hitched there on the fourth of next month—maybe we won't."

Grandma asked, "Why not?"

Uncle Paul answered, "Because if the flood goes on, the water'll reach the church. When we came home today, we went inside to see the minister about something. He was busy taking up the carpets and putting them in the organ loft to keep them from getting wet."

"Well, aren't there other churches in Portland?"

"Not as far as Miss Withington is concerned," said Uncle Paul, sloshing more gravy on his potatoes. "She was christened in Trinity Church."

Miss Withington sounded forceful, like Maud Williams. I guessed Allan liked the kind of woman who told him what to do. I wondered if Lorelei Withington was red-headed too.

SHE WAS A DARK BLONDE with a wide chin and bulging blue eyes. She sat next to Allan in the parlor of the Withington mansion on a dark blue love seat. Her hair was up in a smooth pompadour. Her dress was light blue toile with an Irish lace bertha, pale blue ribbons, and a lace ruffle at the bottom. She was posing on that blue love seat just like Jocelyn did in a basket of quilting scraps. I didn't like her the first minute I laid eyes on her, and I didn't take to the other Withingtons either.

Mr. Withington was a big man with a big nose, big stomach, and bald head. He had the most important cough I'd ever heard and the biggest gold watch I ever saw. He kept looking at it all the time, giving me the impression he wished we'd all go home. Mrs. Withington was little, but inclined to be fat like Lorelei, and her voice was loud. She wore dull blue silk with jet beads all over the front and sleeves. Jerome was yellow-haired, but weedy. He had on a fancy purple velvet suit with knee pants and a dangling cravat, and he sat on a blue stool next to his mother, staring at me.

I'd thought the Lamberts' house was elegant, but it couldn't hold a candle to the nabob banker's place. The country might be suffering from bad times, but the Withingtons weren't. Everything that could have gold on it did. The furniture was covered with light pink and blue and pale gold brocade. Where Aunt Beulah had one houseboy, the Withingtons had two, who brought us drinks as fast as our glasses were empty. I was scared to death I'd spill pink lemonade on my chair. Even Grandma sat stiffly. Oh, she was impressed all right. She didn't dare to snort out loud. Mama spoke only when Mrs. Withington asked her a question. I kept quiet also unless I was spoken to. I imagined how Mama must feel. The clothes we had on were fine for parties and church socials in Oysterville, but not for

Portland where ladies wore gowns made by Worth in Paris, France. Aunt Beulah had told me that Mrs. Withington was dressed "exclusively by Worth."

While Lorelei snuggled Allan and stared at me over her champagne, Mrs. Withington asked me, "Amanda, where do you go to school?"

"Nahcotta, ma'am."

"Is that a public school?"

"It sure is."

"Lorelei attended Saint Helen's Hall," said Mrs. Withington. "She studied Music, Art, Latin, French, Elocution, and Deportment."

I gave Lorelei a quick look. From the way she was lolling on Allan, I guessed she hadn't gotten A's in Deportment. Maybe the rest of the Barnetts weren't good enough for the nabobs, but Allan surely was.

Mrs. Withington turned to Grandma next while I took another glass of lemonade from the houseboy. "Mrs. Barnett, where did you say your family came from?"

Allan burst in with, "Which side, the one with the in-laws that were outlaws?"

Nobody laughed but me. They all stiffened up, except Jerome, who put his hand over his mouth and bent forward on his stool, covering up a laugh. I decided there might be some hope in him after all.

"Why, Allan, you know perfectly well there never have been any outlaws among the Barnetts at all." Grandma leaned forward to speak to Mrs. Withington. "The Barnetts hail from Kansas and Missouri—before that from Ohio and before that from western Virginia. I heard tell the first

Barnett came over from England about 1790. Now my side of the family, the Courtneys—"

Mrs. Withington interrupted. "Then the Barnetts were too late for the American Revolution?"

"If the Barnetts hadn't been too late, they'd have been on the side of the British," Allan joshed some more. I decided he was really getting devil-may-care, the way Mrs. Hankinson said he would when he got married.

The banker's wife plowed on, ignoring him, though Jerome had chuckled out loud. "My husband's family came over on the *Mayflower*. Mine came to Massachusetts four years later."

I wanted to ask what kept them home that long, but didn't. I kept my eye fixed on Jerome, who kept his fixed on me.

Once we'd settled who had the oldest ancestors, Mr. Withington started in on Mama—how many acres of land did we have, how much livestock, and did we own oyster beds? He didn't seem too impressed by what she told him. Grandma was looking sour. I should have been glad, but I wasn't, not when it was the Withingtons who made her look so cross. I didn't like being out among the nabobs at all.

To build us up, I said, "Grandmother wins the blue ribbon at the quilt contest at the County Fair almost every year."

"Every single year!" Grandma corrected me.

"So far," put in Allan softly, winking at me.

Mrs. Withington paid no attention to him. She laughed. "Oh, Mrs. Barnett, we don't make quilts anymore in Portland. That's terribly countrified and passé! We do petit point."

That made Grandma even more sour. And it stopped the conversation. I didn't try to break the long silence. I kept listening for the Withington telephone to ring. Maybe they hid it so far back in the great big house they had a servant who did nothing but sit next to it, waiting for it to ring.

Finally Lorelei spoke up. Turning around in her love seat, she said to her mother, "I'm sorry, but Amanda simply will not do!" She waved her hand toward me. "She's entirely the wrong size, Mother, too big and gawky to be a flower girl and too short to be a bridesmaid. What's more, the carnation pink I've chosen for the bridesmaids wouldn't become her at all. With her yellow hair color, the pink would simply wash her out to nothing."

Mrs. Withington pursed her thin lips and Lorelei pouted, both giving me a good once-over. I was mad as hops, not because I was too big or too little, but because they didn't give a hoot what I thought or how I felt. I was glad I didn't have to be in the old wedding, and I was glad I'd worn my pink muslin dress that washed me out.

"Jerome's too big, too, to be a ring bearer," Lorelei complained.

"Hurray and hallelujah!" shouted Jerome. Then I knew he was on my side.

Mrs. Withington stared at her son. "Yes, I do believe I see what you mean. It is a pity, but Jerome has grown. We need two quite small children. I'll try to find them."

"Hire midgets," suggested Allan. "There's a midget act at the Marquam Theater."

"Allan, do be serious." Mrs. Withington smiled at him, showing all of her teeth, which were mostly gold. Then she started talking about the opera company staying at the Portland Hotel longer than they'd planned because of the flood and what a "cultural" community Portland was getting to be. "We have a box at the theater," she told Mama. "The eve of the wedding we shall all go to the opera."

"Not me," said Uncle Paul, his first words since we'd come to the Withingtons.

"But it's *Carmen*, Paul," exclaimed Aunt Beulah.

"I don't care if it's cabdrivers, Beulah. You know me and opera."

All the Withingtons chuckled, even Mr. Withington, who was looking at his watch again. Aunt Beulah just sighed. I knew what operas were and loved singing, so I said, "I never saw an opera, but I like to hear people sing songs. That'll be fun!"

"Opera is never fun, child!" Mrs. Withington informed me. "It is uplifting in some cases, in others educational." She gave Uncle Paul a sly look. "And for some it is a hopeless cause."

That ended the evening. We all stood up. Lorelei grabbed Allan. When he kissed her on the forehead, she let him go. We went down to Uncle Paul's carriage, with Mrs. Withington right behind us and Lorelei hanging onto Allan's arm, dragging him along. Jerome winked at me from the porch. I decided to have a talk with him as soon as I could.

Nobody talked on the way home except that Mama said she hoped Ching didn't have his hands too full minding Horace while we were gone. When we piled out of the carriage, I asked Allan up to my room. After a while he came.

"Golly, Allan, are you really going to marry that Lorelei?"

He sat on my bed. "It looks that way, doesn't it?"

I plunked down next to him. "But you liked Maud Williams better." Then I told him a whopper. "She was really broken up when Grandma told her about you and the banker's daughter."

"Was she?" He looked interested, for the first time all evening. "What'd she say?"

I couldn't think of anything, so I said, "She wept."

He turned mournful, then shrugged and asked, "Hey, Amanda, how are you coming along with that red rose quilt for Mrs. Hankinson?"

"We're up to the last red, and she's sewing along fine." I didn't want to talk about O the Red Rose Tree and get sadder. I wanted to settle up with the Withingtons.

"Oh, Allan, I wish you wouldn't marry Lorelei. Not because she doesn't want me in the wedding. The Withingtons aren't just nabobs. They're great big snobs. Mrs. Withington is *awful*. She's even too much for Grandma."

"Uh-huh, I noticed that, too. Well, they're like most other Portland folks I've met, except for Uncle Paul. You can't expect people to be the same the world over, Amanda."

"You can, too! I'll bet the nice folks are!" I hollered at him. "You've gone to the dogs. You're devil-may-care now."

He got out just before I threw my hairbrush at him. I went over to the window seat that faced southeast and looked out at the Willamette. The moon was more than three-quarters full, and the river was wide and silver-smooth. I almost wished it would come up and wash me back to the Peninsula. The lantern lights of boats were like the gold candle flames on our Christmas tree at home.

I opened the window to hear the boat whistles, but instead I heard someone knocking on my door. I hoped it wasn't Grandma, scolding me for something I did wrong at the Withingtons' or for my fingernails being dirty or my table manners.

It was Ching. He bowed to me. "Ching heard Missy Barnett yelling at big brother. Missy Barnett hungry? Want something from kitchen before bedtime?"

"No, thank you." As he smiled and backed away, I suddenly thought of Lee Bing Hung. "Hey, do you know somebody named Lee Bing Hung in Portland?"

For a second I saw his eyes get wider. Then he said, "Not know Lee Bing Hung." He shook his head very hard from side to side.

"Well, I guess I'll have to go down to Chinatown and look for him," I said. "I have some news for him about the Boss in Ilwaco. Where is Chinatown here?"

"On Pine Street and Second Avenue." He added, "Not good place for girl to go. Chinatown flooded."

"Oh, pooh, I can row a boat just fine."

"That not what Ching meant. Missy Barnett must not go to Chinatown alone."

"Because of highbinders with throwing hatchets? Grandma says Chinatowns are full of them."

He sighed. "Missy Lambert get angry if Missy Barnett go to Chinatown alone."

"Because of the highbinders?" I asked again.

"Sure." Ching sighed again. "Hundreds of highbinders there throwing hatchets. Thousands of highbinders! Besides, girl going to Chinatown not nice thing to do!"

Rats! That'd keep me from going alone to Chinatown all right. I'd ask Allan to take me, but I didn't think we were speaking anymore.

# 8

# *High Water!*

I DID A LOT of thinking that night about how my brother had changed. He acted as if he didn't care about anything much anymore. It was because of Maud Williams. His heart was broken. As soon as I could get Mama alone, I'd ask her if she didn't think so too. Mama was gentle and she was quiet, but she knew her oats about people.

Mama didn't come down to breakfast, though, and neither did Grandma. Aunt Beulah said they were tired from the trip and so was Horace, who was sleeping longer than usual. I didn't think Mama was so much affected by the trip as she was by the snobbish Withingtons. I hoped Grandma was lying in bed plotting revenge against Lorelei and her mother, but I doubted that. She'd swallow her pride to help Allan catch a banker's daughter, so she could brag to the ladies of her sewing circle.

Aunt Beulah and I had breakfast alone. Uncle Paul and Allan had left for work in downtown Portland already. "You and I are going shopping this morning, Amanda," she told me. "I need scarves for the yellow breakfast. I've invited eight ladies and have only six scarves."

131

Shopping. Meier & Frank and Lipman Wolfe at last, but I didn't understand one bit what scarves had to do with breakfasts. I put on my pink dress again and a straw bonnet with strawberries on it that Mama had got for me in Astoria, and was ready to go.

Portland was hot and sticky. Mount Hood, a vanilla pudding if ever I saw one, was showing clear in the east, but the sky to the west, toward the ocean, was gray. "Oh, dear," said Aunt Beulah, "I think we may have a storm. We certainly don't need more water in town right now."

We took the carriage to Meier & Frank on Second and Taylor. Aunt Beulah had wanted to go to Olds, Wortman & King first, but that store, which was on First Street, was probably underwater. Oh, Meier & Frank was interesting! I never had seen so many things for sale in one place at one time. The store even had "departments"—ready-to-wear clothes for girls and boys, dishes, jewelry, furniture, clocks, and everything under the sun a person could ever want. Aunt Beulah couldn't match her scarves, however, so we went to Lipman Wolfe. There she found the scarves and bought them. Then we went to the ladies' clothing department on the second floor. I'd seen enough. Shopping made a person tired after a while, particularly if she didn't have any money. Bored of walking and my feet aching, I went to look out the store window at the flood, while Aunt Beulah bought corn-colored creponette tea gowns for Mama and Grandma to wear at the yellow breakfast.

Aunt Beulah asked me if I wanted to go to any particular store department and look around. I shook my head. I'd had a gander at the fabric counters while we were at Meier

& Frank. The price tags on the bolts of red cotton from Germany had made me feel dizzy with hopelessness. There were lots of reds—deep ones, light ones, orangeish and bluish ones—but all priced sky-high. I didn't want to look at any more bolts of red cloth. I wanted to get out of the stores entirely.

I pointed down from Lipman Wolfe's window. "I'd like to see the flood. Let's hire a boat. There are lots of them waiting down there."

Aunt Beulah, who was looking over my shoulder, giggled. "That would be fun, wouldn't it? I'll buy an umbrella for each of us in case it rains."

Oh, she spent money like water. Twenty minutes later we were in a canoe, renting for $1.50 per hour. It was a birchbark with red-and-green striped cushions. The flood was a sight all right, and still rising. Aunt Beulah told me she couldn't begin to guess where all the boats came from, but there were hundreds of them—dories, skiffs, dugouts, sailboats, rafts, whaleboats, everything but a "Venetian gondola," she said. And just then a black-hulled gondola came around the corner of a building on Second Street, packed with people waving their hats and bonnets. An American flag was painted on the stern, and along the sides lettered on bright green bunting was a sign: *The San Marco Opera Company. Held Over by Popular Request and High Water.* The gondolier wore a straw hat with ribbons hanging down and was singing "Santa Lucia" as he went by us.

"Now fancy that. I didn't know there was a gondola in town," exclaimed Aunt Beulah, as our paddler took us to Front Street where the water was deepest. There we saw men going in and out second-story windows into saloons, which had all moved upstairs from the first floor. In one place we saw some men sitting on chairs on a raft drinking beer. They lifted up their mugs as we paddled by. Aunt Beulah and I pretended not to see them.

I nearly fell out of the canoe with shock, though, when all at once a submarine diver came up like a sea monster right alongside us. He looked at me through the glass plate on his helmet and walked heavily over to another boat where some men were waiting with pumps going. Our paddler stopped to watch while the men in the boat opened the diver's face plate. "Give me a cold chisel and hammer," I heard the diver tell them. "I can get the basement safe open with that and the money out."

They gave him a chisel and a little sledgehammer, and bolted back his face piece. Then down he went, blowing bubbles.

"Goodness, fancy seeing that on Front Street!" exclaimed Aunt Beulah.

We paddled on, watching people falling off elevated plank walkways into the flood. I saw an elderly lady drop her purse. Without hesitating a minute, she jumped into the water, holding her nose, and dived down after it. I admired her greatly when she brought up the purse, so I clapped. She looked holes right through me, climbed out, wrung out her skirt, and walked off like nothing at all had happened.

Washington Street was even more exciting because of the fire at the flour dealer's. We watched as two hook-and-ladder companies arrived on scows and the firemen leaped off and moved around in chest-deep water, putting ladders in place and stringing hoses. Even with all the water handy in the Willamette River, the fire went on blazing for a half hour, with the black-snake fire hoses floating on the surface.

More and more firemen arrived in rowboats, yelling when freight barges or wading horses, pulling wagons, blocked their way.

"Good heavens, fancy that—a fire in a flood!" cried Aunt Beulah. Then as a fat raindrop splatted on my nose, she looked up at the sky. "Oh, Amanda, dear, it is going to storm." When we got off on dry land, she grabbed my hand and pulled me along to Couch Street. "This is the Blagen block, Amanda. There's something here you certainly must see before you go home."

If I'd ever known anything wonderful, the steam elevators in the Blagen block were it—lots more wonderful than the radiators or even the telephone! They went from the basement to the fourth floor. I could have gone up and down forever with Aunt Beulah, but the man who ran them was getting sick of us. He told Aunt Beulah on the tenth trip, "You better not come back here tomorrow, ladies. I think we're gonna be out of steam pretty soon."

We took a horse-drawn streetcar part of the way home, but had to get off when the storm struck. We ran for blocks, with lightning flashing all around us and thunder booming from the west. Inside the house it was an uproar, too. Mama was holding Horace, who was yelling murder and trying to climb up a drapery. Ching had his fingers in his ears, while Grandma was scowling in the parlor doorway, her lips moving. We couldn't hear a word she was saying because of the telephone. It rang and rang. It never stopped long enough for anybody to count the bells. Aunt Beulah ran to it and took the thing people heard through off the hook and let it dangle, which didn't do one bit of good. The bell kept on ringing as the lightning flashed.

"It's always this way in an electrical storm," Aunt Beulah screamed into my ear. "The only thing to do is ignore it." Then she grabbed Mama and Grandma by the elbows and dragged them into the parlor and shut the doors.

"Beulah, this is a madhouse," said Grandma Barnett. "That instrument is a horror."

"Sometimes it *is* a mixed blessing, Mother," said Aunt Beulah, taking off her sailor hat and putting it down on a table. She took her bundles from me, opened the parcels from Lipman Wolfe, and showed them the tea gowns. "They're presents for you, to be worn at the yellow breakfast tomorrow."

Mama said, "Ooh, thank you, Beulah." While Horace made a grab at her gown and Mama hauled him back, Grandma lifted hers up and looked at it through her spectacles. "Beulah, you know I never did care for yellow. It's a jaundiced color. And the gowns are identical."

"No, they aren't quite the same. Yours, the big one, has lilies of the valley at the breast. The smaller one has Johnny-jump-ups." Aunt Beulah wasn't buffaloed one bit.

Grandma didn't give up. "Beulah, these are tea gowns. They're for afternoons at home. Nobody wears tea gowns to a breakfast!"

"They do in Portland, Mother. My breakfast will start

at three o'clock. That's 'afternoon' and we shall be 'at home.'"

Grandma's jaws clamped shut like a turtle's, then she looked at me. "What's Amanda to wear?"

"The yellow silk dress I bought for her for her fourteenth birthday. Allan helped me pick it out." Aunt Beulah put her arm around me. "I'm giving it to you now, Amanda. If you'd like, you can wear it to the wedding, too."

"Thank you, Aunt Beulah" was all I said. I knew I wasn't going to be a bridesmaid and have to suffer in the pink Lorelei had picked out, but I hoped I wouldn't have to go to the wedding at all.

"My, you don't seem happy about it, dear," my aunt told me.

I said right out, "I don't like the Withingtons!"

"But, Amanda, they're some of the best people in Portland. We introduced Allan to Lorelei, ourselves."

I looked at Mama. From her face I could tell she agreed with me, but she said, "Amanda, it's Allan's business. He'll do as he likes."

"And that Withington girl's a real catch!" added Grandma.

"If I caught her, I'd throw her back," I flared, and ran upstairs to my room. I'd rather be back digging clams in Allan's rolled-up overalls than be out among the Portland nabobs in a silk dress, even if I'd never had one before.

The yellow breakfast was bilious, and not only because the Withington ladies were there. Aunt Beulah had gone hog-wild. The draperies in the dining room were drawn, and pale yellow glass lamps covered the lighted gas jets.

The table was set with yellow damask, yellow china, and gold-plated flatware. In the center were hothouse daffodils. The eight big yellow scarves were thrown over the green dining-room chairs to cover them. Aunt Beulah wore a plush gown the color of buttercups. Grandma and Mama were in their corn-color tea gowns and I was in my new yellow silk dress, which was a little bit too tight across the chest. Of course, the Withingtons came in yellow too. Lorelei even had a wreath of little yellow roses in her hair. The breakfast was "golden buck," cheese poured over poached eggs on toast, and tea in gold-colored cups with lemon wedges on the side. The ladies had sauterne wine while I had milk. I couldn't eat more than two bites. Neither could anybody else, though I noticed they drank the wine.

They could sure chatter, though. The flood was interesting to me, and maybe dangerous too, but the ladies didn't talk about it. They talked some about the opera company's "clever gondola" and the extra operas they'd be playing in Portland because they couldn't get down to San Francisco on account of the flood. But mostly they gabbled about the wedding.

Lorelei was plenty sour. Trinity Church was flooded because of yesterday's rainstorm. The wedding was only two days off, so probably it would be postponed.

"But, darling," said one of the Portland ladies, "there are other churches on higher ground."

Lorelei scowled. "But I've always planned to be married there."

"And so you shall be. We shall wait," said her mother. She turned to Grandma Barnett. "Will you folks be staying on with Beulah until the waters subside?"

I guessed from her tone that she'd be happy if we country people left before the nuptials. But Grandma fixed her wagon good. "Oh, yes, we don't marry off a Barnett every day. And it will be some time before dear little Amanda marries Reverend Pratt's son. They're a lovely Peninsula family."

Kissin' John? Me—marry him? I'd drown myself in a crab hole before I'd do that. Wait till I told Molly and Jessy and Pheemie about Grandma's horrible plot against me. My stomach gurgled with anger while the old lady on my left, who had a pug dog on her lap with a yellow ribbon around his neck, asked Lorelei about the wedding plans.

"I really shouldn't tell," said Lorelei coyly, "but I will. The chancel will be a mass of roses and the altar just covered with buds. There'll be garlands of roses on the gas fixtures."

"What color roses?" I asked, figuring it was time I said something, or blew up or threw up.

Lorelei blinked her eyes at me, surprised. "White ones, of course. I have decided on white orange blossoms over my veil. My maid of honor will carry white roses."

"Men like red roses better than white ones," I told her.

"Red roses are vulgar," said Mrs. Withington. "And when it comes to weddings, it doesn't matter what men like." She gave me that be-silent-child look, which made me glad I wasn't Jerome. He must lead a terrible life. I looked over Mrs. Withington's head at Ching, who held the yellow teapot ready to pour. He was grinning at me. He understood. I grinned back.

THE NEXT AFTERNOON I got to know Jerome at last. Without any warning, Allan came home early from the bank, bringing Jerome with him.

"Come on, Amanda," Allan said. "You and Jerome and I are going to have some fun today."

"Doing what? Catching carp and salmon out of second-story windows downtown?" According to the *Oregonian*, people were doing just that.

"Nope, seeing a regatta."

"What's that?" I had no intention of making up with him so easy.

"A sort of show of boats and a race that the Chinese are running. Their companies own the boats."

I decided I might forgive Allan a little and go. After all, he was helpless. Lorelei's clutches were probably tight ones. She was mighty forceful, like her mother. "Highbinders?" I had to know that before I went.

"Good lord, no," said Jerome. "There aren't many of them in Portland. Papa says the Chinese are the sharpest businessmen in town. He lends them money, and they try to get the lowest interest they can. They're tough customers, but they aren't highbinders."

"They like to gamble," added my brother. "I've bet a five-dollar gold piece on one of the company boats."

Gambling! He'd gone to the dogs and was devil-may-care all right. But I went to the regatta with him, and why not? Nobody in the family was home. Aunt Beulah, Mama, Grandma, and even Horace had gone to tea at the Withingtons'. I hadn't been invited and was glad of it.

Ching came to the front door with us. "Where Missy Barnett go now?" he asked me. "Missy Lambert will want to know."

"To the races in Chinatown," I told him.

"Have good time," he said. "Beware of highbinders!"

I was still laughing at his parting words when we left the streetcar at the water's edge of Sixth Street. There Allan hired a rowboat and ordered, "Take us to Second to the Chinese regatta. And don't bump any boats. This boy with us can't swim."

I looked at Jerome with pity. "I can play the violin," he told me.

"I can play the piano a little bit. Swimming's easy, Jerome."

Our rower tied his boat to an awning bolt on a building next to a Chinese newspaper pasted on the wall. I wanted to talk to Jerome about the wedding and his sister, but couldn't because of Allan. And because of Jerome I couldn't talk to Allan about how awful Lorelei was. So we discussed the flood and Jerome's school, an academy for boys. I decided I liked him in spite of his velvet suits and was going to admit it, when I heard a loud gonging sound.

"They're coming," said Allan. "Keep your eyes peeled. They'll start at the police station here on Second and go up to Sixth and Oak and come back. They'll make the run twice."

"That's quite a way," said Jerome, standing up.

"Sit down in a boat," Allan ordered, taking a watch out of his pocket.

The gonging got louder. Then the first boat came into view, followed by nine others like it, except for the colors of the paddlers' silk shirts. The big boats carried from five to eight paddlers, a steersman at the stern, and a man in the middle with a gong and stick to keep time. As the paddles lifted up out of the dirty water I could see the Chinese letters painted on them in bright colors.

"I put my bet on the crew in the orange shirts," Allan said. "They're in the boat the company calls *Fragrance of Sweet Happiness*. What boat looks good to you, Amanda? Do you like the blue shirts or the black ones?"

Coming from the Peninsula, I was a judge of good boat work all right. I could row and scull as well as any boy I knew. I watched how easily the racing boats dodged other boats in their way and lined up in front of a stone building across the street. A derby-hatted man, leaning out of the second-story window, shouted to the company boats, "Line up straight now!"

"That's Detective Griffin," Allan explained. "He's the official timekeeper for the race."

I listened to the men hanging out of windows, yelling and screaming in Chinese. Some of them waved paper money at each other. I guessed they surely were gamblers, but that didn't seem to stop the police from helping with the race. The detective in the police-station window fired a pistol into the air. Off went the Chinese boats, all at the same time, smooth as glass. Everybody cheered and I cheered too. I'd decided I liked the boat with the orange-shirted rowers. They knew their oats and got the lead right away. Allan had been right.

"Have you got anything to bet me, Amanda?" Jerome suddenly asked.

"No, ladies don't bet." But I would have if I'd had anything with me except that old comb with two teeth missing, which Portland nabobs wouldn't want.

We sat waiting while the gonging grew fainter and fainter and the yelling died down. And then when it was more quiet, I heard something—a sort of hissing. I looked around. The hissing was coming from a little skiff behind us. I poked my brother in the back so he'd turn around and look too.

There was Lee Bing Hung sitting alone in the boat. Neither Allan nor I twitched a muscle, though we were right under the eyes of the Portland police. Lee Bing Hung rowed up beside us. "Missy Barnett, Lee hear you got news for him."

Ching had given him my message! I said quickly, "The Boss at Ilwaco, he's all right. He's just fine. Dr. Perkins said so."

Lee Bing Hung smiled from ear to ear. "Good news. Lee glad to hear. Thank you, Missy Barnett."

Allan stuck out his hand and they shook hands.

"Boss mean man," Lee Bing Hung told him. "Hit Lee before Lee hit him and keep Lee's money."

"We know what he was like," said Allan.

Lee looked away from Allan to Jerome. Knowing what

he was thinking, I said, "Oh, Jerome's all right. He's a friend."

Lee Bing Hung grinned again. "What you do with old red rag I trade you for on beach, Little Missy?"

"Put it into a beautiful quilt, at least I hope it'll turn out to be a quilt."

Lee feathered his oars and started away. "That good! Good-bye, Barnetts."

I called after him, "Are you getting rich?"

"Lee bet ten dollars today on *Fragrance of Sweet Happiness*. They going to win that make Lee plenty rich." Then he disappeared beyond a building corner. I was glad his troubles were over and that I'd helped him, though mine seemed worse than ever, and I was wondering if we'd ever get back to the Peninsula again because of the danged postponed wedding and the flood.

"Hey, who was that?" Jerome wanted to know.

"Somebody we used to know down on the Peninsula," Allan explained.

Jerome seemed surprised. "Amanda, how'd Lee know you had news for him? How'd you get in touch with him?"

"I told Ching to tell him that I was here in Portland."

"Well, I never thought of doing that," said Allan. "I forgot all about Lee's coming from this neck of the woods. I guess I wasn't thinking very straight."

"I don't think you've thought at all since you came up here," I told him, not caring if I made him mad.

Jerome busted in. "Hey, listen! The gong's getting loud again. They're coming back!"

The orange shirts were out in front of the green shirts. They came flashing down the flooded street while people shouted their heads off. I'd been told the Chinese were quiet, but they were louder yellers even than the white men. *Fragrance of Sweet Happiness* swept by the detective, who looked at his watch and bellowed, "Five minutes and thirty seconds!" Then the boats splashed past the police station onto the second lap.

"Look," I told Jerome, "I've got a comb with two teeth missing. That's all I've got to bet."

"Who're you betting on?" he wanted to know.

"The orange shirts!"

"I was picking them, too, Amanda."

That took care of that. I sat in the rowboat, listening to the Chinese going on at a great rate above my head, talking, laughing, and crying out to each other. Allan wasn't paying one bit of attention now to the race. He was looking melancholy while he dabbled his fingers in the muddy flood water. I guessed it was too late to save him.

So I gave him the whole truth. "Maud Williams didn't weep one bit when Grandma told her your news. All she said was 'That's nice.' "

"That's about what I figured she'd say."

I tried to comfort him. "She didn't say it as if she liked saying it, though."

"It doesn't matter anymore, Amanda."

A few minutes later *Fragrance of Sweet Happiness* came back, gonging like mad, to win the race. While the Chinese howled and yelled and handed each other fistfuls of money, a man rowed over from across the street and paid Allan the money he'd won. Allan pocketed it without a smile, so I knew he was really feeling low.

"Tonight's the opera," Jerome reminded us. "We've got to get home."

Though the wedding had been postponed until "after the flood," it seemed we were going to the opera all the same.

"Have you been to many operas?" I asked Jerome, as we rowed to Sixth Street.

"Uh-huh. Some are worse than others. *Carmen* isn't too bad. Singers are pretty fat most of the time, though, and they aren't good actors either, Amanda. Mother says they have big chests so they can sing well, but I think it's because they eat too much."

I liked Jerome Withington. He called a spade a spade and not a dirty shovel. "You're pretty smart for a city kid," I told him.

"I like you, too, Amanda. I knew I was going to get along good with you when you didn't want to be in my sister's wedding either." He whispered, "Hey, sometimes I get to go behind the scenes and meet the singers. My mother's in the opera association."

"You do! Do those Italians talk Italian to you?"

"No, they talk English. But mostly my mother talks to them."

"I can sure understand that."

"Mother's a real talker, Amanda."

"I've noticed."

"Well, your grandmother doesn't take any blue ribbons!"

"Oh, yes, she does. She takes all of them she can get."
I wished I could share my deep dark secret about O the Red Rose Tree with him. He'd understand, but he might tell his mother or sister, and they'd tell Aunt Beulah, and she'd probably blurt it out.

"What do you Portland folks wear to operas?" I asked.

"Your best clothes and all your jewels, I guess."

That would be easy for me, with Aunt Beulah's yellow silk dress and my little cameo pin. I laughed as our boat scraped up onto the sidewalk of Sixth Street. "I'll even wash my neck for the opera, Jerry."

"I won't. I wasn't even going to wash to be in the wedding," he informed me, as we got out of the boat.

I grabbed his elbow while Allan paid the rower. "Jerry, do you want your sister to get married to my brother?"

"Gosh, no. I like Allan. *I* sure wouldn't marry my sister!"


BEFORE I GOT DRESSED for the opera I talked with Ching in the hallway beside the telephone, which seemed to be resting from all its hard work yesterday. "I saw Lee Bing Hung. Thank you, Ching. Everything's fine now. How'd Lee know where to find me?"

"You tell Ching you go to boat race. I call Lee Bing Hung at joss house. I tell Lee Bing Hung look for Missy Barnett and big brother at race."

"Oh." Then I asked him, "What do you think of my brother?"

"Very fine fellow."

"Do you think he ought to marry Miss Lorelei?"

Ching's face went blank. "Not Ching's business."

I knew when I'd reached a dead end and changed the subject. "Ching, have you ever been to an opera?"

He grinned. "Ching go to opera in Chinatown in San Francisco."

"What're they like?"

"Very fine. Many people die, but Chinese opera always end happy. Student passes examination. Young lovers marry."

I sighed. Life certainly wasn't like that much of the time. I'd failed lots of tests, and Allan was marrying the wrong girl. "Are the operas the Italians give like that, too?" I hoped they were. I needed something to cheer me up.

"Ching not know. Mr. Paul say everybody die at end. That one reason why Mr. Paul not go."

Then the telephone rang, and we stopped talking. I counted in English while Ching counted in Chinese. Over the seventh ring, he said, "Telephone yell at me! Must go!"

That evening Aunt Beulah and we Barnetts piled into the carriage, dolled up fit to kill, and drove off to the opera. Horace stayed behind, with Uncle Paul and Ching, which worried Mama a little, but Grandma told her that Horace would be just fine. He'd broken two vases that morning and pulled the heads off half the flowers in Aunt Beulah's garden. He ought to sleep like a top.

The Withingtons were already in their box at the Casino Opera House when we arrived. Mrs. Withington was all in brown silk with amber beads up the front of her gown.

In her hair were bronze plumes, held up by tortoiseshell combs. Mr. Withington was in a black tailcoat, and Jerome in a black velvet suit, this time with a ruffled shirt. Lorelei wore lilac crepe with lilac bows on her shoulders. On each side of her head were little white bird wings. I'd never seen anybody look so putrid.

"Oh, darling, you've come à la Viking. You look good enough to eat," Aunt Beulah told her.

With those wings on her head, I thought Lorelei looked like a sea gull that had gone through a gale, but I kept quiet. My chair was a spindly little gold-painted thing placed next to Jerome's in the front row of the box where the grown-ups could keep an eye on us, but I had a good view of the opera house. The box was on the left side of the theater right above the stage. The curtain was dark blue velvet trimmed with silver; the seats below were blue-cushioned.

Mrs. Withington, Jerome, and Aunt Beulah had pearl-handled opera glasses. I looked through Jerome's at the people filling up the opera house. I couldn't see that the flood had kept many Portland folks at home; either that or they all lived on the west side of the Willamette above the water. One of the ladies who'd come to the yellow breakfast and her husband had the box next to us. She and Grandma started talking about who had the oldest ancestors, but when the black-coated orchestra came out and took their places below the curtain, Mrs. Withington hushed both of them with a loud "sh-h-h."

The orchestra leader had a lot of hair, which shook all over when he slammed the stick down on his music rack to make the orchestra stop talking. His beard quivered while they played a piece that was so fast I wondered how the musicians kept up with each other.

"What was that?" I asked Jerome.

"The overture. It always comes first in an opera."

Lorelei hit us with her fan. "Shush, children."

We both gave her dirty looks, which she ignored. Then the curtain went up, creaking most of the way to the top, stopped with a jerk, and came down partway again. I was not deceived by what I saw. The scene was supposed to be a street, but it was painted on a flat screen. There was a bridge in the background, a big building on the left and another one of a different color on the right. The people were real, though. Some men in funny-looking black hats and yellow coats were standing bunched together on the left. Other men in black clothes and shawled women were milling around them in circles, not knowing which way to go.

"It's a street in Spain. People are out promenading," Jerome whispered. "Those are soldiers in the yellow coats."

All of a sudden the soldiers started to sing, but I couldn't understand one word. "What're they saying, Jerry?"

"It's in French. I don't know."

"A street in *Spain* and they're talking in *French*!" I would have said plenty more about how silly that was, but just then a heavyset blonde with pigtails and a blue skirt came on stage. She sang in a high pretty voice. The soldiers sang back at her. One of them, a short, portly one, sang to her more than the others like he knew her.

Then a thing happened that made Grandma snort so loud the people in the boxes on either side of us turned to stare. A whole bunch of women had come on stage all at once, dressed in green and purple and yellow skirts, flowered blouses, and black shawls over their shoulders. It wasn't only that they were strutting with their hands on their hips with men following them. The ladies were all *smoking*!

"Hussies! Scandalous!" I heard Grandma say to Aunt Beulah.

"Oh, hush, Mother. They're Spanish cigarette girls. They make cigarettes in that tobacco factory, painted on the right."

Because I'd never seen a "hussy" before, I kept close watch on them. From the right a woman walked on. Everybody clapped and clapped, and some men shouted. Through Jerome's opera glasses I could see why. She was beautiful, black-haired and not at all fat. She had on a fringed shawl of many colors and a short, black skirt that showed lots of black net stocking and low-cut black shoes with high scarlet heels. Between her white teeth was a rose—a red one!

"That's Carmen, the wicked gypsy girl," Jerome told me.

When the clapping stopped, Carmen started to sing. Her voice, low and throbbing, made my spine curl. She sang to the portly little soldier, too, flirting with him. I surely couldn't see what both the blond girl and the gypsy saw in him. All the while Carmen was flirting with him she twirled the red rose in her hand. Finally she tossed it in his face, whirled around, and ran into the door of the tobacco factory. I came out with a loud "My goodness!" When

Carmen had whirled, the black skirt belled out over her petticoats, and I'd seen the top one. It was red—fiery orange-red, and it hadn't gleamed one bit. I'd bet a whole double eagle, if I had one, that the petticoat was cotton, not shiny silk or taffeta.

I heard Grandma behind me. "You're quite right, Amanda, to say 'My goodness.' This play is extremely morally bilious and not at all suited for children."

"Mrs. Barnett, do be silent. We want to hear the fight in the factory." Mrs. Withington's voice had icicles hanging from it.

# 9

## *Bellini*

A FIGHT! I loved fights. I watched through Jerome's opera glasses to see if I could get another glimpse of the gypsy's petticoat. There ought to be some running around in a fight. I got two good looks—one when Carmen ran singing to slap another cigarette girl and the other time when she pushed down the soldier everybody loved and ran away laughing after he'd arrested her. Carmen had real spunk!

Then the curtain came down. "That's the end of Act One," Jerome told me.

I could hear Grandma Barnett whispering to Mama about the "low nature" of the opera. I thought *Carmen* was just wonderful, and oh, that red petticoat!

"You know, Jerry, 'Where there's a will, there's gotta be a way,' " I recited from my sampler.

"Huh?"

"Did you say you can go back where the singers are?"

"Yes, but I don't know if Mother'll go tonight." He looked over his shoulder at Mrs. Withington, who had a vinegar expression on her face. "She's getting mad at your

153

grandmother, Amanda." He pulled his chair closer to mine. "Do you want to go backstage? Do you want to meet Bellini?"

"Who's Bellini?"

He shook his head at my dumb question, then opened his program. On page seven, after a whole bunch of advertisements, he showed me the words: Carmen . . . . Rosa Bellini.

"Oh, sure, she's the wicked gypsy. She's the one I want to see. Do we have to take your mother along?"

"No, she'll stay here while Papa and your brother buy ices in the lobby for all the ladies and bring them back. We'll leave during the Intermezzo."

"What's that?"

"The music the orchestra plays between Act Two and Act Three."

"All right, we'll go then." I kept my eyes on Carmen all during Act Two but her costume was different now that she'd left the cigarette factory for a place in some mountains in Spain, where she was supposed to be a smuggler. She didn't really need to wear the red petticoat then. Finally the curtain fell down, and Jerome and I got up together.

"Where do you think you are going?" asked Lorelei.

"To get a drink of water," said Jerome, sticking out his tongue at her to show how dry it was.

We went out of the box, down back stairs, and out into a dark alley. Jerome didn't have to stop to get his bearings. He went up to a door at the top of some steps, opened it, and went inside. We were backstage now, which was a big mess full of large, flat painted screens, piles of rope, barrels, racks of costumes, and people. I saw some of the singers close up without their black wigs on. They weren't gypsies at all, not swarthy one bit. It was all paint. The blond lady in the blue skirt wasn't even a real blonde. She held a wig in her hand while she drank tea.

Nobody paid any attention to us. Jerome led me down a narrow hall to a door with a white star painted on it. He knocked, and a lady's voice called out, "Enter."

We went in. Because of lots of gas lamps, the little room was bright, and was it ever in a clutter—clothing all over the chairs with baskets of flowers and fruit piled on top. The room smelled of perfume, flowers, and black cigars. Carmen herself sat in front of a mirror, a different shawl over her shoulders, putting a red rose in her real black hair.

"What you want here, little boy?" she asked Jerome, looking at his reflection in her mirror.

While he told her who he was, I saw *it*, half buried under a dozen red roses—American Beauties, I supposed. The petticoat was redder than the roses, and it *was* cotton!

Jerome introduced me. "This is Amanda Ann Barnett, Miss Bellini. She wants to meet you."

"I am pleased to meet you, *signorina*," said Carmen.

I figured the Intermezzo wouldn't be any longer than the overture, so I spoke right up. "I didn't really want to meet you, Miss Bellini."

"What?" She turned around, her mouth open.

"No, it was something else." There was a little stool with some calla lilies on it. I brushed them onto the floor and sat down. As fast as I could I told her about Mrs. Hankinson, how poor she was, how lonely, how she'd wanted to make a special quilt with red roses in it for sixty-three years, and how I needed one last red.

She listened, frowning, then asked, "And you come to Bellini for help, eh?"

"Oh, yes. I need the red petticoat you wore in the first act."

She gestured. "Take it. It is mine. I give it to you for a good deed. It makes Bellini happy." She pulled an enormous pink peony out of a vase on her dressing table and handed it to Jerome, who did an astonishing thing. He bowed and kissed her hand, and she smiled.

I had my hands on the petticoat and was about to say thank you when the door opened. In came a man. He had white hair and a black moustache and wore evening clothes just like Mr. Withington's and Allan's. Looking at his watch he said, "Four minutes, Rosa, *cuore del mio cuore.*" Then he spied us. "Who are these children? What are they doing here?"

Bellini laughed. "Aldo, go away. I am giving them gifts."

"What this time?" he asked, still holding the watch.

"The flower to the charming little boy, the petticoat to the girl."

The man stepped forward and jerked the petticoat out of my hand. "The flower, yes. The petticoat, no. It is opera company property, Rosa, you give no more away!"

"The petticoat is *mine*, Aldo Corallo."

"It is *ours!*"

Bellini was on her feet, every inch of her a Carmen. Her dark eyes flashed at him. His dark eyes flashed at her. She picked up a cold-cream jar, shouting, "Manager of the company, do not forget you are Bellini's husband too. *Mostro, bruto*, skinflint from Genoa! This little girl does a good deed for a poor old woman. *Ti odioso!*"

Jerome and I backed up toward the door and only just in time. The cold-cream jar went whizzing by Corallo's head and smashed against the dressing-room wall. Bellini had a big cardboard box of talcum powder in one hand.

Corallo yelled at her, "*Cuore del mio cuore*, little idiot from Naples. You will bankrupt us with your giving. I'll teach Bellini to obey her husband." He lunged for the dressing table and picked up her hairbrush.

"Bellini obey a *husband!* No. *Mai, mai*, never." Powder box ready to let fly, she went on shrieking in Italian while Jerome and I got the door open and ran out, dashing for the alley. We stopped there, panting.

"Are all singers from Italy like that?" I asked.

When he got back his breath, he told me, "Some of them are just naturally, but Papa says some are because that's how Americans expect them to be." He leaned against the wall. "Gosh, Amanda, I heard what you said about that old lady down on the Peninsula. Why didn't you tell me you wanted red cloth? I'd lend you the money."

"Nope." I'd thought about this too. We'd gone along so far without asking anybody for money, so I wouldn't now. "Jerry, I couldn't pay you back for maybe years and years." I patted him on the back. "Thank you, but I can't. You know, I almost got the red petticoat."

"Tell me some more about Mrs. Hankinson and the quilt," he said, as we started back toward the box. When

I'd finished, he nodded. "I sure hope you all get it done in time, and the old lady gets the blue ribbon. And don't worry about my telling anybody about your secret and seeing Bellini." Dumping the peony in a cigar stand outside the Withington box, we took our seats just as the curtain went up.

Sadly I watched the rest of the opera. Carmen and the short soldier quarreling in Act Three. And in Act Four, the soldier, who was called Don José, stabbing her to death with a knife because she'd been untrue to him with the handsome, loud-voiced bullfighter. Carmen hadn't worn the red petticoat again. I guessed it was still in her dressing room, buried under roses.

When the clapping was all over, Grandma said loud enough for everybody nearby to hear, "I think that was the most shocking thing I have ever seen. Amanda should never have witnessed it."

"It didn't hurt me, Grandma." Rats! I knew how awful life could be. Allan spoke up, the first time all evening. "Well, buck up, everybody. We're all going to Podesta's for supper. I've made the arrangements."

Mr. Withington coughed. "It's on Third Street. That's underwater, son."

"I checked on it. They've moved upstairs," Allan told him. "We'll go in through a window."

"Oh, darling, it will be a lark!" exclaimed Lorelei.

"Well, I don't know," put in Grandma.

"Don't be a dry stick, Mother," said Aunt Beulah. "The best Portland people are going in and out of second-story windows these days. Mr. Withington and Allan will help you."

I liked Podesta's better than I'd liked the last sad hunk of *Carmen*. Now I knew what Uncle Paul meant about operas. Don José would have to die, too, because he'd stabbed Carmen. Podesta's had red candles stuck in wine bottles and red-and-white checkered tablecloths. I liked the spaghetti that Allan ordered for us. It came in long white strings covered with red sauce. Mama, Grandma, and I didn't know what to do with it until Allan showed us how to wind it up on a fork.

I was just starting through the spaghetti when all the waiters in the place suddenly began clapping and yelling, "Bravo! Bravo!" Then I saw Carmen, or Mrs. Corallo, or Bellini, or whatever she called herself, come through the window across the room, pulled in by the mean, white-haired man. Oh, how beautiful she was in a long evening cape with diamond-studded combs in her hair. Under the cape she was dressed in shining black satin trimmed with jet and pearl beads. She looked around the restaurant, saw Jerome and me, and waved and smiled back. Even Grandma was impressed and didn't say a word about her being a "hussy."

I was the last to finish eating because the strings were so hard to catch and fell off the fork as fast as I wound them up.

When I'd chased my last string of slippery spaghetti around my plate, Mr. Withington sighed and said, "I'll get us a boat."

"Get two boats," ordered his wife. "I hate being crowded."

I noticed Mr. Corallo getting up at the same time and going to the window that folks used as a door. He gave Mr. Withington a fierce look and wouldn't step aside. "Boat! Boat!" he called out.

Mr. Withington shouted over Corallo's head, "Two boats wanted!" Then he crooked his finger for all of us to come on. Allan and I went to the window next to the entrance window and looked out on the flood. The moon was almost full, bright as a five-dollar gold piece, and the night was almost as clear as day. Two boats were being rowed over, only two.

Bellini came to the window, giggling, and stuck her head out next to mine. A big cloud of perfume floated around her. "The water is deep?" she asked Allan.

"It's over your head, ma'am."

"But there are only two boats. We have to have three for all of us to leave," complained Lorelei from another window.

"You watch. Aldo will get one of the boats. The man with the great fat stomach will not get both," Bellini confided in me.

Meanwhile, the opera manager and the banker were struggling to see who'd get out of the window first and grab a boat. Both had big stomachs that got in the way, though Lorelei's father's was bigger. Corallo got out first, after knocking Mr. Withington to the floor, and stepped down into a rowboat. Then he lifted Bellini down after yelling at her in Italian to hurry up, I figured. Next Mr.

Withington, mad as a hornet, got down into the second boat. He yelled, "Amanda, Jerome!" and held up his arms. I went out the window and was lifted down by him, more or less. He rocked the boat reaching for me, grabbed me by the knees, and over the side we went together. Oh, the Willamette was cold!

When I came up, spitting out water, I saw Mr. Corallo standing in his boat, laughing fit to bust, pointing a finger at Mr. Withington, who was thrashing around in the water while the rower of his boat kept yelling, "Grab an oar, mister. Hang on to it. Hang on!"

Corallo's laughing at us got my goat plenty. Everybody was watching the banker grabbing for the oar, so I dived down and swam underwater to the opera manager's boat, went under it, and came up on the other side. I grabbed the gunwale, and gave the boat a sudden jerk, and over it went, tipping everybody out into the flood.

The two rowers were hollering. I looked up at Podesta's. The people hanging out the restaurant windows were yelling bloody murder too. Bellini was screaming in the water next to me. Everybody was making noise except Mr. Withington, who'd lost hold of the oar, and Mr. Corallo who hadn't come up at all.

Bellini took a lungful of air, treading water, and sang out, "Save Aldo! My husband cannot swim!"

Quick as an arrow Allan went jumping out the window. He bobbed up beside me, gulped air, and dived.

While he was underwater, Mrs. Withington called down, "Allan, save my husband. He can't swim!"

I treaded water next to Bellini and waited. This was

horrible! What had I done! Finally Allan came up, his hands tangled in Mr. Corallo's white hair. He towed him to the Withington boat, where the rower grabbed him by the collar and held his head out of water. The other rower, who was swimming, got Mr. Withington before he went down again.

"Aldo is saved?" Bellini asked me, her hair hanging down in strings around her face.

"Yes, my brother saved him."

Then she did an odd thing. She swam over to her husband, who was coughing up the river, stared into his face, then motioned to me and pointed toward the stairs nearby that were mostly underwater. She swam to them and climbed up to the top step. I followed her up the stairs where nobody could see us.

"Little girl, I give you the petticoat for saving my Aldo!"

I watched her pull up her black skirt to the top of the petticoat, untie it, and drop it into the flood. "Put it on," she ordered.

With her help, we got it on under my skirt. "Thank you. Oh, thank you. What'll you tell your husband?"

"That the drawstring broke in the water and it floated away. My combs are lost, too!"

She hurried down the steps, swam out, and got hauled back into Podesta's by waiters. Then I got pulled inside, too, where Mr. Withington and Mr. Corallo were sitting, wrapped in tablecloths. Waiters stood ready with glasses of brandy. Allan was in a corner surrounded by Withingtons and Barnetts and Aunt Beulah, wringing her hands.

Instead of telling him how wonderful he was, the Withingtons were going at him!

Raking the air and stamping her feet, Lorelei screamed, "Why didn't you save my father first instead of that foreigner?"

"You saved that dreadful Italian before Mr. Withington, even when I called down to you that he couldn't swim!" accused Mrs. Withington at the top of her lungs.

"How could I hear you when I was underwater?" asked Allan calmly.

"Yes, how could he?" Grandma threw in.

"You shut up!" Mrs. Withington turned on her.

"You shut up, yourself!" flared Grandma.

Aunt Beulah had her fingers in her ears, while Mama had backed away against the wall. Jerome was sitting in a chair, his eyes sparkling while he chomped on a breadstick.

"I hate you, Allan Barnett!" Lorelei exploded, bursting into tears. "I wouldn't marry you if you were the last man on earth—not ever!" She took the engagement ring off her finger and threw it into his face just the way Carmen had done to Don José in the last act before he stabbed her in the brisket. She ran to her father, followed by her mother. Jerome, who still had the breadstick, slowly trailed after them.

I caught him by the coattail as he left. "Thanks for everything, Jerry." Then I whispered into his ear, "Bellini had the red petticoat on. She gave it to me because Allan saved her husband. Honest, if Allan had known your pa couldn't swim, he would have saved him first."

"I know, Amanda," Jerome told me. "I'll call you on the telephone later on."

Mr. Withington had recovered enough for waiters to help him down into a boat now, and the whole family left out the window.

We all sat down together at a table, even though Allan and I were sopping wet. Grandma looked furious, Mama sad, and Aunt Beulah upset. But Allan seemed almost happy. He was smiling to himself. And I certainly knew that I was happy—happy as a clam! I had Carmen's petticoat for O the Red Rose Tree and Allan back again.

"Oh, dear, Allan," said Aunt Beulah, "Mr. Withington will fire you at the bank."

"Oh, my Lord, I didn't think of that!" exclaimed Grandma.

My brother spoke quietly. "He can't fire me, Beulah, I just quit. People in Portland are just too peculiar for me. I think I'm over my restless spell. I'll go home to the Peninsula and join the Life Saving Service. I guess shipwrecks ought to give me all the excitement I'll ever need."

I flung my arms around him, happier than ever, hugging him while flood water from both of us ran all over Podesta's floor. It had been the most wonderful evening of my life, and the finest flood I'd ever seen!

Even more wonderful, Mr. Corallo sent over a bottle of wine to our table. Then, at Allan's invitation, he and Bellini joined us. Aunt Beulah was absolutely wild with joy. She whispered to me that it was the "social triumph of the summer." Even Grandma was pleased to have a famous singer sit with us.

Bellini pretended she'd never met me before she came to Podesta's, but around midnight she asked me, "Little girl, what do you want to hear me sing for you?"

Sing? The only song I knew that was Italian was "Santa Lucia."

Her long black hair hanging down to her waist, she got up on a chair and sang it to us, while one of the waiters accompanied her on an accordian. Then she kissed me on the cheek and Allan right on the mouth, calling him a "handsome hero" and making him blush. I guessed he'd never forget that night either!

THERE WAS STEAM HEAT in the radiator in my bedroom at Aunt Beulah's when I got back. I dried the red petticoat over it during the night. It was color-true, all right, as I'd figured. Although my yellow silk dress was ruined by the water, there were no red stains on it from the wet petticoat. When the petticoat was dry, I packed it secretly in the bottom of my suitcase.

We stayed only a couple of days longer, for Allan to settle some business he had in town and to sell his houseboat, which was still floating somewhere in downtown Portland. Jerome called me on the telephone, so I could say I'd talked over it. He sounded just like himself, even when he hiccuped.

This time with Allan along, we boarded the *T.J. Potter* again, homeward bound, thank heaven. Aunt Beulah rode in one of the rowboats with us to say good-bye. She'd told me privately that she figured the Withingtons would be friends with her and Uncle Paul again after Allan, "that thorn in the Withington side," had gone. Nobody was mad at her anyhow. I was glad for her.

"Come back and visit again, Mother, when the flood's over and the gas is on again," she called up to Grandma on the deck.

Portland hadn't had any gas for thirty-six hours. People had to get along with coal-oil lamps like we did all the time on the Peninsula, poor things!

Grandma waved her handkerchief. "Come back here to that madhouse of yours, Beulah! Yellow breakfasts, nabobs all over the place, Italian gypsies, smoking women, canceled nuptials, and that awful, awful telephone. It'd be a real catastrophe that'd bring me back to Portland again!" She went off to her cabin, muttering, while the *T.J. Potter* cast off and swung around, heading down the Willamette for the Columbia River

"I never thought it'd happen, Amanda, but Grandma met her match in Mrs. Withington," Allan told me.

"I'm glad you didn't meet your match with Lorelei," I joked. He laughed. Then I told him about the red petticoat Bellini had given me for O the Red Rose Tree.

He'd remembered her costume in the first act, all right. "How'd you ever get *that*, Amanda?" He looked shocked.

"Mostly by crook, I guess." No, I wouldn't tell him any more, particularly how I'd upset Corallo's boat when nobody was looking. I'd tell Jessy Reed, though. We were even in wickedness now, and it wouldn't be fair of me not to let her know.

Pa was certainly glad to see us back home again. He said

he was sick of bacon and eggs, which was all he could cook, and he was lonesome, too, with only cows to talk to. He was glad Allan had escaped the banker's daughter, who didn't sound like any "bargain" to him. And he laughed fit to kill when Mama told him about the opera and the supper afterward. He asked Grandma straight out, "What'll you tell the good ladies in your sewing circle about Allan's coming home single?"

"That the Withingtons took Amanda to a dreadful stage show and had no shame at all about it. That *Carmen* was simply full of hussies."

"Morally bilious, huh? I figured you'd have a dandy answer ready for 'em, Ma," he told her.

I kept quiet except for yelling as I tried to keep Edward T. Bone and Horace apart. The dog wanted to lick Horace's face. Horace wanted to kiss Edward T. Bone, who was as glad to see us back as Pa was. It wouldn't be sanitary for the dog to be kissed.

"Pa," I asked, after I shoved Edward T. Bone out onto the porch, "have you seen Pheemie or Molly or Jessy or Dr. Alf or Nurse Williams or Mrs. Hankinson?"

"I haven't seen a soul, Amanda, but Preacher Pratt the Sunday you were gone."

That took care of that. There wasn't any news then. The next morning I got up earlier even than Pa, ate a piece of old biscuit, and with Carmen's petticoat under my arm hotfooted it to Pheemie's house. She was always up before anybody else even when school was out for the summer, like now, so she could be alone with her pa's horses and be first to see if any one of them was sick. And she was always ready to go on an eerie walk if I showed up unexpectedly.

"Hey, Euphemia," I called under her window, after I'd given my sea gull sounds.

When she stuck her head out upstairs, I unfurled the petticoat. In the rays of the sun coming up, it had the color of sunset before a storm. Her eyes bugged out. "Gosh almighty!" She jerked her head back in, bumping it on the window frame. She came down in her nightgown and grabbed the petticoat to look it over. "Golly, Amanda! There's enough here for all seven roses if we'd only got hold of it first. How'd you do it?"

"I'll tell you when we're all together. What's happened here while I've been gone?"

"Oh, a few things. Did Allan get married?" Pheemie asked mournfully.

"He never did! He came back with us. He's going to join the Life Saving Service at Klipsan Beach."

Pheemie was sour, "And live in the station where Molly does, huh?"

"Nope, I think he'll start courting Miss Williams and try to marry her. That way he'll live with her in a little house on the beach. Euphemia, give him up. He's too old for you, and he needs a strong hand on his check rein." I figured that'd warn her about him and not keep her hoping. "What's new here?"

"Well, I found a red, too," she told me.

"Where? Did you give it to Mrs. Hankinson?" Had I gone to all that work in Portland for nothing?

"No." She shook her head and led the way to the barn, where she always kept her bib overalls, which she put on now over her nightgown. "It was the lining of a man's vest I found in the Indian village at Bay Center and traded some candy for. Some summer tourist had traded it to the Indians for baskets, I guess. Well, it was cotton all right. It didn't bleed in cold water in the horse trough, but then I tried it in hot water just to make sure. Gosh, did it ever bleed and shrink then! It had a funny smell too."

I nodded. "I guess it must have been an off-breed of dye, huh?"

"It wasn't Turkey red, Amanda. It sort of stunk like turkey feathers burning, though."

"Well, this petticoat from Portland doesn't bleed one bit. Come on, let's show Jessy and then Molly and then go on down to the silver shack with it. It's early enough to be a good eerie walk along the way."

By eight o'clock we were all on our way together to the silver shack, and then, glory be, something else nice happened. Along came Dr. Alf and Miss Williams in the buggy. They both looked worn down to nubbins. Rosinante looked better than they did. When I grabbed her bridle, Dr. Alf barked out, "Amanda, let go of that animal. We've been up all night at the Pratts'. It's twins, two baby girls this time."

I wasn't interested in the Pratts except to wonder if looking after two babies wouldn't cramp John's style. Horace sure cramped mine sometimes. I whipped out the red petticoat from under my arm and waved it in the breeze at the buggy. Rosinante shied. Dr. Alf blinked at it and shaded his eyes with his hand. "My God, what's that I see?"

"The great Bellini's petticoat from *Carmen*. It's the last red!"

He shuddered. "Whoever it belongs to, it's too early in the morning to look at a sight like that. It gives me vertigo."

I ran around to Miss Williams' side of the buggy. "Hey, my brother Allan's back. He didn't marry the banker's bilious daughter."

"Why not?" asked Dr. Alf.

I took a deep breath and kept my eyes on Maud Williams. "Because he did not love her. He gave his heart to another first."

"She's got red hair and lives in Nahcotta," put in Jessy.

"At the Palace Hotel," added Pheemie.

"He's going to join the Life Saving Service and stay here," Molly told them both.

Miss Williams knew what we meant, but she didn't say a word. She smiled a little, though, as Dr. Alf ordered, "Now, Amanda, you release this horse at once." I had hold of the bridle on the nurse's side now.

"Just one question first. How's the boss of the cranberry pickers?"

Dr. Alf looked puzzled. "Just fine, I guess. I haven't seen the ornery old devil in weeks. I didn't know you cared, Amanda."

"Is he still out to get even with the young man who hit him?"

"No, the Boss wanted to press charges, but when we heard the circumstances of the attack, we talked him out of it. Now take that wild petticoat down to the Hankinson place and bedevil somebody else."

"We will. Thank you! Thank you!" I was so happy I danced up and down in the road ruts, flapping the petticoat. Lee Bing Hung was off the hook all the way.

Rosinante got so flustered by the flapping that she whinnied and broke into a trot. Pheemie stood looking after Rosinante as she went down the road toward Nahcotta. "You know, there's life in that old mare yet!" she told us. Nobody knew more about horses than Euphemia Sharp.

WE FOUND Mrs. Hankinson making clam chowder, chopping onions and potatoes. She had the chopping knife in her hand when she came to the door, but she dropped it on the floor when I held up Carmen's red petticoat and shook it in her face.

"Land a mercy! Look at that, will you?"

We led her to a chair and sat her down while Molly picked up the knife and finished the chopping. I put the skirt in Mrs. Hankinson's lap and told her the whole story of *Carmen*, Rosa Bellini and Mr. Corallo, and the Portland flood—everything but my tipping over the boat. I finished with, "Bellini wanted you to have this to put in O the Red Rose Tree when I told her you'd wanted to make it for over sixty-three years."

As she smoothed the red cloth, I saw how gnarled Mrs. Hankinson's hands were and how they trembled, more than ever now. Her voice trembled, too. "Oh, girls, that's nice to hear. A singin' lady wanted me to have her petticoat. I'd rather have it from a singin' person than anybody else.

Oh, girls, you've all been so good to me. I come down here to die 'cause I had no place else to go and look what happened. I find four friends." A tear started down one of her cheek wrinkles. "I got to be honest with you, though. There ain't gonna be any O the Red Rose Tree after all."

"*What?*" cried Pheemie.

"How come?" wailed Jessy.

Mrs. Hankinson held up her shaking hands. "I can't work fast enough with these hands anymore. There's too much sewin' left to do before the Fair. The last rose and the rest a the leaves I can do mebbe. But the quiltin' and the turnin' of the corners, I can't do all them things. Girls, I bit off more'n I can chew. I'm sorry." She looked down at the petticoat spread out like fire across her old black skirt. "I'm sorry but it ain't so much the place you set out for, it's the travelin'. That's what my husband used to say, and he was dead right. I been happy travelin' here, happier than I ever been except when I was back home with him and the young'uns."

"Were we too late with the reds?" I had to know.

"No, Amanda. It ain't you being slow. It's me, like I just told you. If I had had all them reds to start out with, I still couldn't do it. In my younger days I could a got it done easy. I'm too slow now. I'm just too old and my hands pain me bad sometimes and I got the shakes. Mebbe for next year's Fair it'll be ready, but I just can't do by September all that still has to be done."

I wanted to break down and bawl. All the strain and work for nothing, not to mention crookedness! I looked at Bellini's petticoat, wondering what the opera singer would say if I told her this bad news. Then I heard Molly's voice.

"Don't you fret. We'll do it, Mrs. Hankinson!"

"Who's 'we'?" shouted Pheemie.

"You and Amanda and Jessy and me. We'll do the quilting and turn the corners."

Rats! Molly'd struck again. Grandma always claimed that quilting and turning was the meanest work there was in quilt making. I looked at the quilt frame in the ceiling. The sword of Damocles had just dropped on us. "Forty thumbs! Forty thumbs!" I whispered to Pheemie.

Mrs. Hankinson reached out to pat Molly's arm. "Thank you, Molly, dear."

# 10

## A Real Red Red!

I HAD PLENTY in mind to say to Molly outside but didn't, because I saw Pheemie's and Jessy's faces before I opened my mouth. They were all looking daggers at me. I guessed we were going to sew O the Red Rose Tree even if it was going to be a disaster. I told myself as I trudged home that there wouldn't be any fun at all that summer, just sore fingers and needle pricks.

I WAS RIGHT. The only one who enjoyed the summer was Allan. He joined the Life Saving Service and went to live in the surfmen's quarters of the big station, but I heard from Jessy that he spent lots of time in Nahcotta. She saw him going in and out of the Palace Hotel all the time and in a buggy hired from the livery stable, driving Miss Williams through town. I figured they were both goners. Buggy riding three times led to wedding bells—that's what Mama told me once when we were discussing Life. And when Allan came home sometimes to Sunday chicken and dumplings, he sure looked happy. Even Miss Williams smiled sometimes when I saw her.

I wasn't smiling. I was sewing and suffering every morning down at the silver shack. To cover up, I told Mama and Grandma I was working on another sampler now that I'd finished "Where There's a Will, There's a Way!" That explained the state of my fingers too.

Mrs. Hankinson set the quilt by the end of July, sewing everything she'd appliquéd together onto the white muslin. And now came the hard part for us. We pulled down Allan's frame, got out the sheet and batting I'd bought in Astoria, and pinned the set quilt over the batting, which had been put on top of the sheet. Now for the first time we got a good look at O the Red Rose Tree laid out flat.

"Ooh," Molly breathed. "It's beautiful!"

"Sure is," said Pheemie, while Jessy was speechless, probably because she couldn't think of any book quotation that fit.

It *was* beautiful. The roses, all different reds except for the two out of Grandma's union suit, looked just fine together against the three different greens of the jaggedy leaves. Bellini's petticoat made the biggest, prettiest flower of all, right in the center of the tree. A full-blown rose, it looked like a real flower except that it was a foot and half across. There'd been plenty of petticoat and leaf cloth left over to make a green and red border to match the quilt. We girls helped piece and sew the border onto the top edges of O the Red Rose Tree and then struggled half of August, folding the border over and sewing it onto the backside of the quilt. Turning those danged corners was the meanest part of all so far. The corners were where the judges really looked. Each of us girls did one, and we were all scared when we worked at it, not only because of the judges. Another reason was that Mrs. Hankinson had told us, "Bad corners mean somethin' bad is goin' to happen. Them corners have gotta be good. I've already done somethin' that ain't supposed to be lucky in this quilt."

Jessy stopped threading her needle. "What's that?"

"Not puttin' in a blue leaf or mebbe a green flower."

"A green rose? Who ever heard of that?" hooted Pheemie.

"Lots a quilt makers, Euphemia. Folks back home say if a thing's too fine, it makes old split hoof jealous and mean, and he gets even by bringin' bad luck." I didn't think Mrs. Hankinson looked too unhappy, though. She'd sung dozens of songs to us while we sewed, and now she started on one I'd never heard, about the "knight of old" who met the devil along the road.

When she was done singing, Molly asked, "Couldn't you have squeezed in a blue leaf, a tiny little one?" She had stopped sewing to reach down and pet Jocelyn, who was rubbing his head against her skirt.

"Nope," said Mrs. Hankinson. "I wanted O the Red Rose Tree perfect. Now, girls, don't fret about it. Don't forget what I told you—don' take no more'n three stitches at one time, and keep up your count of no more'n eight of 'em to one inch. Hitch 'em tight and don' never backstitch!"

All the rest of August we quilted, sewing in a crisscross pattern over the top of O the Red Rose Tree through the batting down through the sheet. The quilting held the batting tight inside and kept it from lumping up in places. Quilting was the worst work I'd ever done in my whole life, lots harder on my back than digging clams. I went at it like killing snakes, but carefully. I thought that the quilt would never get done. At night I even dreamed about stitching and heard Mrs. Hankinson's soft voice and her cough.

But on the twenty-eighth of the month it was finished, in time for the Pacific County Fair on September the third. When Molly took the last little stitch, we all collapsed around the frame, too tired even to yell hurray.

"Who's going to take it to the Fair?" Pheemie wanted to know.

I knew I couldn't, not if I was going to keep O the Red Rose Tree secret from my family. And Allan couldn't take it and enter it either, now that he was at the beck and call of the United States Government.

"I'll do it," volunteered Jessy. "Pa's going up to South Bend day after tomorrow on business at the courthouse. He'll take it to the Fair if I ask him to."

"How'll you keep it secret from your folks?" Molly asked, while Mrs. Hankinson was across the room feeding Jocelyn.

"Easy. I'll take it home wrapped up in the brown paper Amanda bought the cloth in at Astoria. I'll tell Pa and Mama that a sick lady in Oysterville gave it to me to enter in the Fair. They'll never even see it." She scowled as she looked at her fingers, which had little red marks all over them, like mine did. Not one of us had ever been able to use a thimble worth a darn. "You know what, I think I'm getting sick of secrets. Secrets can be a real strain on a person!"

I had to agree with her on that.

"All right, Jessy, you take the quilt, and we'll all see it at the Fair," said Pheemie. She told Mrs. Hankinson, who'd put the kettle on to make us mint tea, "I've already talked to my folks about it. We'll come get you in our buggy the day the Fair opens and take you to the boat and to South Bend."

Mrs. Hankinson gave her a little smile. "No, Euphemia, I'm not goin' to the Fair. You go for me. It's too much of a trip for me, all the way up there and back. I don' want no more sea air neither. It ain't done me any good." Then she looked at me. "Amanda, I know what's goin' on in that head of yers. I'm *not* goin'! You remember, it wasn' O the Red Rose Tree, it was the makin' of it. Thank you for that. Thank you all."

JESSY ENTERED O the Red Rose Tree under the name of Sarah Ann Hankinson of Nahcotta, Washington. She said it had to compete with nine others, not counting Grandma Barnett's Women's Christian Temperance Union quilt Pa'd taken to South Bend for her.

ON THE THIRD of September all of us Barnetts, except Allan who was on duty, headed for Nahcotta. We boarded the little steamer *Shamrock* and rode eight miles in windy weather across Willapa Bay, then steamed up the Willapa River, six miles to South Bend, a good-sized sawmill town.

Jessy, Pheemie, and Molly and their folks were aboard the *Shamrock* too. The minute the steamer dropped her gangplank we girls were off and running toward the fairgrounds.

Jars of mincemeat and pickles didn't interest us and neither did prize-winning chickens and hogs. We ran right past them in the big, drafty fair building to the Art Exhibit where the quilts were. Even from a distance we could see O the Red Rose Tree hanging up on the wall next to another quilt. We'd gone to enough fairs to know that meant a prize for sure!

But not the blue ribbon! Pinned to the lower right corner of our quilt was a red one. *Second prize!* The blue ribbon was pinned to Grandma Barnett's green-and-white quilt. I just stood there with my friends, staring, knowing how bad they felt because I felt the same way.

A tall lady in a wide hat with peacock feathers sprouting out of it stood in the booth where the quilts that hadn't won any prize were piled up. I supposed she was a judge. "How come the quilt with the red roses on it didn't win first prize?" Jessy asked her. "It's the prettiest!"

"Because of the corners, little girl. Unfortunately, there were some crooked stitches on them, but you're right. It's the prettiest one here, a brand-new pattern, but there's no escaping the fact that the green-and-white one has better corners."

"Are you in the WCTU?" demanded Pheemie.

"No, dear, I'm not."

Hearing that didn't make me feel better. It was our corners then, and there was no escaping the truth. While we stood looking mournful, people from all over the fair building came crowding up to the quilt section. I saw Mama and Grandma walking toward us, along with Jessy's mother and Molly's. I thought it would be smart of us to leave, but we were rooted to the sawdust.

Grandma was grinning as she leaned on her cane and gazed at her blue ribbon as if she'd never had one before. Then her eye fell on O the Red Rose Tree. She went up to look at the card pinned to the left side. "Sarah Ann Hankinson," she read out loud so everybody could hear. "Oh, well, it's only second prize."

Well, that took the rag off the bush for us. Jessy exploded, "That's only because Molly and Euphemia and Amanda and I sewed the corners because Mrs. Hankinson was too feeble to do it."

Oh, what a muttering started up now from the crowd. Mama said, "Oh, my!" Grandma swung her head around like an angry cow's to stare at me. Then she said, "Amanda, you helped that dreadful Hankinson woman? You, my own flesh and blood!"

That was Grandma Barnett, all right, jumping on me in front of the whole world! That's why she had such good health, Pa always said. She never held in anything mean that came to her mind. She said it and got rid of it. I was too embarrassed to meet her eyes or to answer her question. I wished I could burrow under the sawdust and disappear.

She went on. "So that's what you were doing all the time down there in the sand dunes? Stabbing me in the back? Where'd you get all that cloth?"

Pheemie told her, "We bought the greens and the white in Astoria for Mrs. Hankinson because we like her."

"The reds weren't half as easy to get," added Jessy, who was plenty mad now. "We got the cloth for the roses just all over. You wouldn't begin to guess where they came from."

Now it was Molly's turn to talk, or rather blurt. "They came out of shipwreck cloth, a chest protector, a doll dress, and a Portland singer's petticoat." She took a deep breath and pointed at Grandma Barnett. "But the two roses on the left side in the same color came out of the front and back of the underwear you got last Christmas!"

Molly Stevens really had done it this time. Everybody started to laugh. I stole a look at Grandma. Her face had gone purple as a pickled beet. She turned on Mama. "I have never been so mortified in my whole life! Mentioning my unmentionables in public! I'll be the laughing-stock of the whole Peninsula from now on. I'm going to Portland to Beulah's as soon as I can pack. I'm taking all of my prize quilts and my blue ribbons and leaving. Don't you try to stop me, Adelaide. It won't do you a bit of good." She glared around at everybody in the quilt booth and particularly at the four of us, then started off with Mama hurrying after her.

When they'd gone, Jessy started giggling. "I wonder if she'll tell your Aunt Beulah why she left the Peninsula, about the union suit she sent her ending up in a quilt."

I felt sort of sorry for Grandma, so I didn't laugh. "I doubt it, Jessamine. Uncle Paul would enjoy it too much.

I think she knows he would, so she'll never let him or Beulah find out."

Jessy's mother, who'd been looking at O the Red Rose Tree close up, came over to tell Jessy that the cloth in one of the rosebuds and one rose looked "mighty familiar" to her. From the look on Mrs. Reed's face, we knew she knew! Now it was Jessy's turn to look at the sawdust and be embarrassed, but when Mrs. Reed heard the story we told her, she laughed and said, "Well, I'm glad to see the chest protector I worked so hard on is in use at last. And now I understand the trick you played on your father and me. It's all right, Jessamine, you meant well, but don't you *ever* do it again. No more tricks, you hear me."

"Oh, we won't," Molly promised Mrs. Reed. "There'll never be another O the Red Rose Tree."

"There sure won't be. We haven't got the strength," agreed Pheemie after Jessy's and Molly's mothers had gone away to have a gander at the giant Hubbard squash everybody was so impressed with.

The four of us walked out of earshot of the lady judge. I felt absolutely awful. Here I'd betrayed my own flesh and blood and been crooked as all get-out to boot. We'd all been crooked, keeping secrets about the things we'd done that our parents would have hated, like trying to get galloping pneumonia and using people's presents for quilt scraps. We hadn't begun to tell Mrs. Reed the whole truth!

Jessy looked down at the jowls too. "We have been very deceitful and venomous." She was quoting from the latest book she'd read.

Because I'd loaned it to her, I knew the part that followed. "And because of our fearful crimes, we have paid the price."

"Second prize, not the first one," said Pheemie sadly.

"More than that, Euphemia," I said mournfully.

"Guilty consciences," added Jessy. "Should we confess all to a confessor?"

I didn't think we should. "Maybe someday, but not right now."

"We could confess to Mrs. Hankinson," Molly suggested.

I turned on her. "No! She loved making O the Red Rose Tree. Telling her would take the joy out of it for her if she knew how bad we'd been."

Pheemie leaned against the display of canned salmon. "We can't tell her. She's too weak and old to hear the whole truth. And if she did, maybe she wouldn't like us so much anymore."

"She wouldn't like the way we got most of the reds," said Molly, who had tears running off the end of her nose. "We should have been punished, and we are being punished. Mrs. Hankinson mustn't ever know that we were more interested in getting those reds than in *how* we got them. It wasn't the 'traveling' for the four of us, like she says it ought to be for people, it was 'arriving' we cared about. We didn't pay any attention to the 'traveling' at all!"

I put my arm around her. "Oh, Molly, don't cry."

Pheemie added, "Yeah, don't cry. There's a horse down at the end of the hall that weighs 1860 pounds. Let's go see him!"

Molly sniffled. "Seeing a big fat horse won't make me feel happier, Euphemia!"

While Pheemie and I walked behind Jessy and Molly, Pheemie asked me, "Do you think your grandma'll really go to Portland?"

"Maybe. She's unregenerate, you know."

"What does that mean?"

"Look it up in the dictionary!"

"All right, I will if you're too mean to tell me, Amanda. But I'll tell *you* something. If your grandma does go, she'll go by broom, I bet!"

I HAD a horrible two days afterward. Pa and Mama both tore into me and into Allan, too, when they found out he'd known about the quilt and made the frame for Mrs. Hankinson. Grandma had meant what she said. She packed for a day and a half and wouldn't even look at Allan or me. I suffered from pangs of guilt and conscience.

But the worst thing was having to go down to the silver shack and tell Mrs. Hankinson that O the Red Rose Tree hadn't got the blue ribbon.

This time she didn't get up out of her chair to let us in, but called out from inside, "Come in, girls." Jocelyn was on her lap, and she was petting him as if she didn't have a care in the world. She looked at each of us, then said softly, "We didn' take first prize, did we?"

"No," I told her, "we got second prize. Pa'll bring the red ribbon and the quilt to you when the Fair's over in a couple of days."

"We're very sorry," put in Pheemie.

"It was our bad sewing on the corners." Molly was weeping.

"Old Mrs. Barnett got the blue ribbon with her ugly WCTU quilt," Jessy said. "I still think it was pull. One judge told us she wasn't a WCTU member, but we don't know about the others."

Mrs. Hankinson shook her head. "No, girls, it wasn' pull. The quilt just plain wasn' the best one."

"We thought it was," Pheemie told her fiercely.

"Maybe we had bad luck because there wasn't a blue leaf or a green flower," Jessy went on, though she didn't really believe that. "But all the same it was the prettiest quilt there. Even that old lady judge said so. I think lots of folks thought it was the best. My mother sure admired it."

"Well, girls, all that matters to me is that the five of us thought so, though it's mighty nice to hear your mother liked it, Jessamine."

"My mother liked it, too," Molly told her. "And the lady judge said it was a brand-new pattern. She knew it wasn't at all like the other everyday quilts. Maybe other Peninsula quilters will copy it."

Mrs. Hankinson laughed. "That calls for a cup of tea, don' it—real tea, India tea. I got a little bit of it left. Here, Euphemia, you lift Jocelyn off me. He's heavy as an anvil now." Pheemie hauled the black cat off Mrs. Hankinson's lap, so she could get up and go to the stove. From there she cocked her head to one side to look at the four of us. "Hearin' all them nice things about O the Red Rose Tree makes the work you done sewin' it worthwhile, don' it? Mebbe there'll be other quilts for you girls and blue ribbons for 'em, too, someday. But we done the one I always wanted, and that's what matters to me." She had her eyes fastened on me. "Amanda, I said it so often I think mebbe you ought to know by now what I was gettin' at when I kept talkin' about the road and the travelin'. I think all of you know it."

I answered her. "I think we all do. We talked about it at the Fair. It's not so much what you got *done*, it's *how* you did it!"

"That's right, girls. That's right!"

GRANDMA LEFT on the *T.J. Potter* the next day. Pa reported that the last thing she said to him before she got aboard the sidewheeler in Astoria was, "Even that awful telephone's preferable to treachery and back stabbing in one's own home. Allan and Amanda are vipers in your bosom, Charles. See to it that Horace does not turn into one too."

Three days later Dr. Alf showed up at our front door early in the morning without our having called for him. It was raining, a warm September rain, and he took a long, long time wiping his feet on our doormat before he came in. I figured his arthritis was acting up, he was so slow.

"I want to see Amanda," I heard him say to Mama, who'd answered the door.

I was in the kitchen, helping fix sausage and country gravy for breakfast. I came out in my apron while he was putting his derby on our hat rack.

"A cup of coffee would be welcome, Mrs. Barnett," he said to Mama. When she was gone, he told me softly,

"Amanda, Mrs. Hankinson's gone, died this morning at daybreak. It was pneumonia, the galloping kind. She was weak, so it took her fast."

I started to cry, but he stopped me. "There isn't any use in that. She wouldn't have wanted you to. She was old and ready to go. I was with her all night." Pa'd come out of the kitchen, so he spoke to both of us. "Mrs. Hankinson told me that she'd never seen girls like Amanda and her friends. She never had such good company and because of them she did what she'd always wanted to do, make that quilt with all the red roses in it." He smiled as he took the coffee cup from Mama. "You know, Mrs. Barnett, I had a part in that quilt too. For one thing I knew all about its being made. For another, my old chest protector's one of the rosebuds. I saw the quilt at Mrs. Hankinson's. It's a real dandy!" He turned to me. "Amanda, I've already dropped by the Reeds' and the Sharps' to tell them about Mrs. Hankinson's death. I delivered that big black cat to Euphemia. Took him there in a gunnysack. That's what Mrs. Hankinson wanted. Will you go to Klipsan Beach and tell Molly Stevens?"

I could only nod I was so choked up to think I'd never go back to the silver shack again.

Dr. Alf spoke to Pa over my head, "Charlie, I'm the executor of the old lady's estate. She left a handwritten will. It mentions Amanda in it. After the funeral there'll be a reading of it in the lawyer's office in Ilwaco. Now don't get the idea it was my thought to have it read. Wills generally aren't, except in novels, but Jessamine Reed insisted. She thought it ought to be done 'right,' with all the girls mentioned in it present. Jessamine says that's how Mrs. Hankinson would have wanted it."

"We're all in the will?" I asked him.

"You certainly are!" he said, while he opened his watch and we all stood listening to the waltz from Vienna. This time he gave us a treat. He let "The Blue Danube" play all the way through.

MRS. HANKINSON was buried in Nahcotta's little cemetery. The coffin was just a plain wooden box, but her grave wasn't plain at all. Molly and I had seen to that.

Allan was let out of the Life Saving Service early that morning. He and Pa, working together, lined the hole in the ground with tall meadow ferns and evergreen boughs, so there wasn't one inch of dirt showing. Preacher Pratt conducted the services with the four of us girls and Dr. Alf in the front row as "chief mourners," as Jessy called us, because there wasn't any family. When the services were over, we came up one by one and laid our flowers on the ground ready to be put on top of the filled-in grave later on. We hadn't got together on the flowers, but each of us had brought roses. Wild briar roses, pink ones, from Jessy, Pheemie, and me, but Molly's were from her mother's climbing bush. They were little ones, only about two inches across, but they were bright, bright red!

ALL OF US went to Ilwaco on the railroad the next day. We were headed for the lawyer's office, and we were scared. Lawyers made us think of sheriffs!

We sat still on hard chairs next to Dr. Alf with our folks behind us, while the lawyer, a big man with a deep voice, read the will. The silver shack and land and "personal goods" went to Dr. Alfred Perkins to sell "as he sees fit" and the money to be given to the Indians at Bay Center to help them through the winter.

Then came the parts about us. "Who is Euphemia Sharp?" the lawyer asked, looking under the bottoms of his silver-rimmed spectacles.

Pheemie stuck up her hand. "Umm," he mumbled, then said, "Euphemia Sharp, spinster, is to receive custody of Jocelyn for six months of the year only. Who is Jocelyn?"

"Mrs. Hankinson's cat, your honor," said Pheemie. "I've already got him at my house. He's eating just fine."

The lawyer read on, "Euphemia Sharp is to have the quilt named 54-40 or Fight." He looked around again. "Who is Jessamine Reed?"

"I am Jessamine Reed," stated Jessy.

"Jessamine Reed, spinster, is to have a brown, green, and orange quilt named Tiger Lily and Jocelyn for the other six months of the year."

Behind me I heard Pa laughing, then start coughing, but the lawyer went on, "Who is Amanda Ann Barnett?"

"That's me, sir."

"Amanda Ann Barnett, spinster, is to have one quilt, said quilt named Sherman's March to the Sea."

Everybody laughed. I felt my ears getting hot. The Yankee soldier, General Sherman, had marched through Georgia to the Atlantic during the Civil War, and Georgia had never been the same again. "Nobody and nothing stood in the path of the Union Army and General Sherman," according to Miss Coxe.

"Amanda Ann Barnett is also to receive one red ribbon, marked *Second Prize*." The lawyer plowed on. "Who is Molly Stevens?"

Molly squeaked out, "Here."

He said, "A quilt named O the Red Rose Tree goes to Molly Stevens, spinster, of Klipsan Beach."

"Molly!" we all shrieked together.

"Be silent, please. This is a legal matter, and I have not finished," ordered the lawyer. "The other quilts go to charity, as Dr. Perkins sees fit. That's all there is to this last will and testament."

We got up, looking at Molly who was crying and wiping her eyes with Dr. Alf's handkerchief. He told her, "Well, Miss Molly Stevens, it seems you came out best of all. You get the prize winner, though Amanda gets the prize."

Pheemie had a fair soul. "Molly ought to, Dr. Alf. She was the one who promised we'd get the red cloth. But what did Mrs. Hankinson mean when she gave us those quilts? We never saw them, though she showed us some others. I'd have remembered those names for sure!"

He smiled at us. "They were in a packing box in her bedroom, all labeled and ready. They're in my office now. I'll deliver them soon."

"But what do you think she meant?" Jessy repeated.

"I'm not sure," Dr. Alf said, "but I think she was paying tribute to your fighting spirit. After all, you did put in a busy year for her, didn't you? And it wasn't easy, I gather."

"It wasn't easy at all," said Jessy.

"It was nearly impossible," I told him. "But it developed our characters all right!"

"Good." He nodded and reached into his pocket and brought out the red ribbon. "As executor of the Hankinson estate, Amanda, I hereby give you this as part of your inheritance."

I took it, careful not to smudge it. I knew exactly where I'd hang it—on a nail on the stair landing where everybody who came to our house could see it. I'd never win another prize making a quilt, not when I couldn't even get used to wearing a thimble.

Pa and Mama and Horace and I got onto the train, heading for home. After we'd taken our seats, Pa asked me, "Amanda, do you have any idea what Sherman's March to the Sea looks like?"

"No, Pa."

"Do you?" he turned to Mama.

"No, Charles, your mother was the quilt maker in our house." Mama was fending off Horace, who was jumping up and down on her lap, trying to pull the cherries off her hat.

Pa laughed. "She would know all about Sherman's March to the Sea. Paul Lambert told me once he thought my mother went on it with Sherman." He smiled at the two of us. "Peace, it's wonderful, but I doubt if she'll stay long in Portland. She'll get peeved at Beulah and be back by Christmas. But there's some hope. Maybe she'll bear in mind that trying to buffalo you, Amanda, might backfire. Let's change the subject and enjoy the quiet while it lasts.

Amanda, do you know what colors are in the quilt Mrs. Hankinson left to you?"

"No, Pa, but I doubt if there's much red in it. Mrs. Hankinson didn't hold with Turkey red and ground-up bugs."

"Speaking of red," said Pa, "someday you'll have to tell us the whole story about all of those reds you got for her."

I thought before I answered him, "I will, but first you'll have to promise you won't take me to the woodshed with a stick. Not even Mrs. Hankinson ever knew all the things we went through for that quilt."

"That bad, huh?" he said. "Well, Amanda, you come out in the barn someday and tell me. You're pretty big to switch now, but I think you'd better mind your *P*'s and *Q*'s all the same from here on. Nobody ever gets too big for life to knock him down, you know."

"Oh, I know that. It isn't the destination that counts, it's how you get there!"

"My, my!" Pa whistled. "I'm glad you've learned that. Now you know why your old pa ain't rich or famous, or likely to be." He leaned forward as the train jerked north. "How about letting me see that ribbon you were willed?"

I took it out of my purse and handed it across to him. He grabbed it just before Horace did. I watched Pa holding the ribbon to the window so it would get the light.

Mama said quietly, "Amanda, you seem to have learned a great deal from Mrs. Hankinson. Perhaps you'll never be the best seamstress in the world, but I think what she's taught you about sewing will stand you in good stead the rest of your life."

I didn't tell her the other things I'd learned. That could come later when I'd thought more about them and had the right words in mind. Words were hard to find sometimes. Even dictionaries couldn't help.

"I know it's only Second Prize, but what do you think of the ribbon?" I asked Pa.

He handed it back to me, grinning. "You know, Amanda, that's what I'd call a real red red!"

# Author's Note

Mostly because so many children have asked me for it in letters, I've returned to *The Nickel-Plated Beauty* country for a second look and a second book. *O the Red Rose Tree* is not a sequel. It is set in time some eight years later, and it has only two characters in common, Dr. Alf Perkins and his horse, Rosinante.

Like *The Nickel-Plated Beauty*, however, there is much material in this book drawn from reminiscences of members of my mother's pioneer family. For their notes and replies to questions asked about the Peninsula, I am greatly indebted to my mother, Mrs. Walter M. Robbins; my aunt, Mrs. Bert Soule (my Aunt Clara); and to the late Mrs. Alfred F. Rimer (my Aunt Nora). Some of the incidents in *O the Red Rose Tree* came out of their lives, though the time sequence is off. I trust readers will forgive me for now and then juggling dates to fit the action of the book. The Oysterville spelling bee took place in 1895, not 1894, with Mrs. Rimer the winner and the "captain of industry" the loser. There was no prize. Injustice! The lined grave, too, is fact. Peninsula people honored my grandfather with just such a burial in 1919, I'm told. The Pacific County Fair began at South Bend in 1896, and was not current in 1894, as I have it. The term Life Saving Service may be strange to child readers of today. However, Life Saving Service was the name used until 1915 when the service merged with another to form what is now called the United States Coast Guard.

Most of the material about quilts has come from books. The patterns listed, except for O the Red Rose Tree, are real, as are the superstitions I've mentioned. My grandmother, who was a fine quilt maker, died in the 1930s. I own two of her products and examined them for this book, but my real expert is Zoma Henry of the Riverside Public Library Reference Department staff. She deserves my gratitude.

The subject of red dyes in the 1890s is, I found, an extremely technical one. For replying to questions about the dye processes of that day, I must thank several members of the University of California at Riverside Department of Chemistry. The German colorfast dyes were coal-tar (aniline) dyes and expensive in this country until 1917 when the United States went to war with Germany and German patents were no longer observed. Turkey red, so popular with people on the American frontier, was indeed made out of the bodies of Mexican cochineal beetles!

The great Portland flood of 1894 is history, and factual, as are most of my comments about it, including the account of the boat race the Chinese staged. Preparing for this part of the book, I went to Portland's Multnomah County Library and to the Oregon Historical Society. Miss Priscilla

Knuth of the latter was particularly helpful in my quest, coming up with large numbers of photographs of the flood. Mrs. Katherine Payne of the South Bend branch of the Timberline Regional Library was also very gracious to me when I called her for aid regarding the Pacific County Fair.

The playing of *Carmen* was not a part of flood days. Other theatrical presentations were, however. Life went on as ever in imperturbable Portland! I chose *Carmen* and an Italian singer, because as a child I recall one of my aunts saying that many years ago the "thrill of her life" had been hearing the great Luisa Tetrazzini sing in the open-air rotunda of the Portland Hotel, a long-time landmark now demolished to make way for "progress."

The fads and fashions I attribute to 1893 and 1894 are drawn from newspapers and magazines of the day. Yellow breakfasts at 3:00 P.M. were the rage. "Rats" was the slang term of the day. Lorelei Withington's costumes and those of her mother are taken from fashion notes. (For Portlanders only: Meier & Frank was at Second and Taylor in 1894. It moved later to its present location.)

Some very knowledgeable people connected with *O the Red Rose Tree* shall be nameless, such as our doctor who supplied data on how to catch a cold and about arthritis and galloping pneumonia. Our lawyer, who has a children's librarian wife, advised me that wills were not *read* at all except in fiction but to go ahead and "do it in your book." The material on red-and-green color blindness is accurate. People so afflicted see only gray when they look at those colors. The episode in the Reeds' store could have happened. (A color-blind acquaintance of ours once repaired the gray upholstery of his car with shocking pink masking tape and never knew the difference!)

Some sources in print that I used for this novel are: *Portland, Oregon, Its History and Builders* by Joseph Gaston; *The Rose City of the World, Portland, Oregon* by Ruby Fay Purdy; and the *History of Portland. Oregon*, edited by H.W. Scott. Miss Elizabeth Anne Johnson, Head of the Literature and History Department of the Public Library Service for Portland and Multnomah County deserves my particular thanks for finding the above-listed books for me. Other valuable sources used were issues of *West Shore* magazine of 1894 and the Portland *Oregonian*, May through July of that year.

Patricia Beatty
December, 1970